THE PLAYER'S CURSE

Slough   01753 535166   Langley   01753 542153
Cippenham   01628 661745   Britwell   01753 522869

Please return/renew this item by the last date shown.
Items may also be renewed by phone and internet.

www.slough.gov.uk
Slough
Borough Council

LIB/3296/08-12-06

THE PLAYER'S CURSE

A Bella Wallis Mystery

Brian Thompson

WINDSOR
PARAGON

First published 2010
by Chatto & Windus
This Large Print edition published 2010
by BBC Audiobooks Ltd
by arrangement with
The Random House Group Ltd

Hardcover ISBN: 978 1 408 48770 9
Softcover   ISBN: 978 1 408 48771 6

British Library Cataloguing in Publication Data available

Printed and bound in Great Britain by
CPI Antony Rowe, Chippenham and Eastbourne

ONE

Jarnac, in south-west France, is a town made rich by brandy, as even the most casual visit can confirm. The always beautiful, always indolent Charente runs through it and though there is something a little asymmetric about the street plan—perhaps the want of a single grand boulevard or imposing hotel de ville—one glance at the cemetery tells the story of the place. What appears to be a small village of bourgeois houses are in fact the tombs of the great distillers and their families. Some travellers like to poke about a place to get at the essence of it: this cemetery tells them all they need to know about Jarnac. In death as in life, money counts.

*   *   *

The little nun was Belgian and as far as these things go, personable. Sister Mathilde was well known to the shopkeepers and hoteliers of Jarnac as a persuasive and gently insistent seeker of alms. Belgian or not, the French liked her. The handsome donations made to the convent at Easter—elegant envelopes of cash from the distillers and their families gathered up on the altar like plump fish—sprang from the affection everyone felt for the whole community of nuns; but especially the one they called Tilde la Belge.

Every Saturday for the past twenty years she had appeared over the bridge at ten on the dot and begun soliciting the townsfolk's charity,

1

approaching rich and poor alike. An artist from Paris had taken her photograph standing under the catalpa tree in front of Demongeot's *tabac*. In the picture a serious child in pinafores was holding her hand while Tilde in turn held onto the little girl's hoop. This image exactly captured the nun, so much so that giant prints of it were to be found in Demongeot's and several of the other bars about town.

Her gap-toothed smile was much appreciated at the Café Turpin by the quayside, where the sailors met, their open boats moored up alongside. These men, who took the brandy barrels downriver and along the coast to Rochefort, were most likely to see Tilde for what she was: somebody's daughter, as it might be from their own family—a tubby little creature with a gimpy leg, driven into the church as a child by bad harvests and a too-innocent mind.

The weather turns in that part of Charente about the end of March. The mists lift off the river and the sandy eyots grow a pale green fuzz. Within a month, the palm of a hand laid flat against a wall or balustrade will find a faint warmth returned. The raked paths of the municipal walks and gardens lose their orange tint and are dry enough to coat a shoe or the hem of a skirt in dust. And then, sometimes in pairs, sometimes in larger groups, the nuns' tragic guests are led out from the gates of the convent—those who the world has driven mad. The women wear white embroidered surplices, the men tunics and trousers in the same colour, topped by floppy berets decorated with pompoms. It is particularly affecting to see grown men holding hands like children and shuffling along with lowered eyes.

'Why do we do this?' Jane Westland asked Sister Mathilde.

'You don't see how pleased everyone is to see you and how correct their address? Doesn't it make you happy to be out of doors in the good Lord's sunshine? I know it does.'

'You don't know anything. I want to sit down.'

Fitting the action to the words, the tall Englishwoman subsided to the path, her legs stuck straight out in front of her. Mathilde smiled and pulled her up by her wrists. For a small woman she had surprising strength.

'For me it is a pleasure,' she said. 'I enjoy your company and—when you wish to be nice to me—your conversation.'

'About the moles on my body.'

'That was harmless nonsense. I am sure you regret saying all those things.'

They sat side by side on a park bench, with a view of the men fishing.

'Can a curse ever be lifted, Tilde?'

'You must always use my full name.'

'If you have been cursed by a truly evil woman, can God take the harm away?'

'God can do all things.'

'Then can you ask Him to help me?'

Sister Mathilde took one of the Englishwoman's long pale hands and held it between her own.

'I do ask Him,' she said. 'I pray for you every day, you know that. I want you to be happy. When you hurt yourself with knives or pins, it pains me.'

'The Mother Superintendent thinks we are lovers.'

Sister Mathilde had inherited her laugh from her grandma, Edith. It was unbecomingly loud and

3

derisive. She let go of Jane's hand and made a dusting motion (derived from her childhood in Edith's kitchen) as of a woman clapping her palms together to rid them of flour. Or foolishness.

'Oh, you wicked girl! Enough to make a crow blush.'

'If I tell you a name—'

'No, don't,' Sister Mathilde said, suddenly sharp. She had heard this name off and on for ten years, enough to blunt even her kindness. She looked up. A man—it was Jippy from the Café Turpin—stood in front of them with two overflowing ice creams in wax-paper cornets.

'This is M. Junot,' Mathilde explained.

'You are not in a zoo, m'sieu, and we are not animals to be fed,' Jane Westland shouted, knocking the ice cream he was proffering out of his hand. Jean-Pierre Junot glanced at the nun and shrugged. Mathilde noticed with a terrible pang of compassion that he had taken off his stocking cap to approach them.

'You do right to cry,' she said to her charge as he walked away. 'I hope these are tears of shame, Jane. You can be cruel.'

'Write to my brother.'

'That is for the Mother Superintendent to decide.'

'Tell *him* the name.'

He already knows it, Mathilde said to herself, the cornet held in front of her like a tiny torch.

'That bitch's curse has put me on this carousel for ever.'

'Nothing is for ever,' Sister Mathilde said.

Jean-Pierre Junot came from La Tremblade. One night he came ashore and found that in his

4

absence at sea his wife and three children had died of typhus, along with forty others. Since that time, he had never uttered a single word. Yet God, whose mercy was infinite, saw to it that nothing was for ever. In time, everything was made straight.

That night, Jane was very bad, her howling loud enough to be heard in both wings of the convent. There were some nuns who hardly bothered to conceal their contempt for the Englishwoman and her arrogant ways. Every week without fail there came a letter from London, always in the same handwriting. Sister Loelie, the convent's postmistress, made it her business to open these envelopes, for if she did not, they would remain just as they had been put into the postbox at the end of Orange Street.

'Your dear brother cares for you enough to send you letters. Why don't you ever read them?'

'Use them to wipe your fat bum,' Jane replied wildly. The violence and indecency of her speech horrified the nuns, more than the cuts she made on her wrists or the soft flesh of her thighs.

Once or twice a month—as tonight—her name was entered in the night ledger and against it the word: *Méchante*.

'What has the world done to her to merit all this?' Sister Loelie grumbled.

'It is a curse laid on her reason by a wicked woman,' Tilde la Belge explained, perhaps for the hundredth time.

'And you believe all that?'

'Does it really matter what I believe?' the little Belgian asked. 'In the men's wing, M. du Temple believes his wits were stolen by the Prussians and carried off back to Berlin for examination by the

Kaiser. If I say I don't believe him, does it make it any better? It does not.'

'What a saint you are, Tilde.'

'And what a fool you.'

The howling had given way to a persistent drumming. Jane Westland was on her back, pounding the locked door of her cell with her naked feet. The violence of her attack made the air in the corridor outside tremble.

* * *

In London, it was a calm morning, at any rate as to the weather. Bella Wallis's doorstep in Orange Street was decorated by a tiny waif called Rosie Timmings who sat with her chin in her hands, waiting to be despatched to the shops by Mrs Venn, the housekeeper. These errands were urgent but haphazardly organised. The front door flew open and a floury Dora Venn coached little Rosie through another imaginary conversation before posting her off with a shove to her scrawny back. It was all very entertaining to the more raucous neighbours, who sped the child down the street with any amount of chaff and nonsense. Much did Rosie Timmings care. Old Mother Venn had a bark much worse than her bite and if she seemed a bit beside herself this particular day, she had reason.

'You give this bit of paper to *young* Mr Protheroe at the fishmonger's, not his dad, but the young boy with the squint, and you say that Dora Venn sent you. And you can tell him likewise that if it goes on like this, the poor woman will be carted off by the mad-doctors before nightfall.'

Inside the house, it was a day for treading carefully. Towards six, Bella came down in a favourite steel-grey gown and began setting the dining table. In a mild attempt to be sardonic, she brought out the best silver for the occasion, laid on starched linen from her mother's day. The central decoration was a rose bowl stuffed—positively stuffed—with purple sweet peas. As was her habit, half an hour before the arrival of her solitary guest she paid a visit to the kitchen to express her thanks.

These were occasions to be finely judged and in a general way Mrs Venn shooed her and her compliments back upstairs with a few good-humoured grumbles. But on this particular evening she found Dora Venn red-faced and fractious, wondering in a thundering sort of voice what sort of a guest it was who must have Solway shrimps, followed by fish and two meats, followed by Russian salad, peaches in brandy and a summer pudding. No amount of joshing could amend her mood.

'You see me all of a fluster, Mrs Wallis, and that's no lie.'

'I know I can depend upon you, Dora. And you will make Mr Westland, whose menu it is, a very happy man.'

'Yes, and hasn't he been down here every ten minutes for the last two hours getting under a body's feet! I don't know who this great man is that's coming but according to the quantities laid down, he must be a powerful eater.'

'I believe he likes his food,' Bella admitted.

'A circus strong man, is he? I will just point out that we have only the one range to cook on and a

7

kitchen table you wouldn't want to play whist at.'

'I shall get Mrs Poe's girl Elizabeth in to lend you a hand,' Bella suggested brightly, eight hours too late.

'You'll do no such thing,' Mrs Venn declared, bursting into tears.

In the dining room, Philip Westland was jumpy and defensive. Yes, his guest was something of a glutton at table but this was offset by his fame, as Bella surely must acknowledge.

'Is fame completely the right word?' she asked, who until last week had never heard of him.

'Dearest, dearest Bella,' Philip murmured in his most soothing voice, as if speaking to an aged aunt or the village idiot. She noticed that when fussing with the wineglasses, holding each up to the light to inspect their cleanliness, his hands were shaking.

'Are these flowers quite the right thing?' he suddenly asked.

'Touch them and I shall have to kill you,' Bella responded.

There was a commotion in the street outside. A giant of a man, not yet thirty, was alighting from a cab, reaching up to shake hands with the driver. Whatever he might have been saying was obscured by the sort of black beard shipwrecked pirates might sport on desert islands. Half a dozen children, who had been running behind the cab, clustered about him, hopping up and down and yahooing. With the utmost nonchalance, he reached into his pocket and threw a shower of coins into the air. Then, jutting out his mighty beard and tugging straight his waistcoat, he searched for the house number. The rap he gave the front door knocker reverberated the glass in the picture frames decorating the hall.

'Ye gods!' Bella whispered.

When Philip fetched his guest into the drawing room, she noticed a strange thing. He was actually shorter than she had imagined and in truth no greater in height than his host. What made him gigantic was the aura of self-assurance that surrounded him, so insistent that it seemed to block the early evening light. You could say of Dr W. G. Grace, cricketer, that he was a burly man swaddled in his own importance. The piratical beard was the consolidation of this effect, as if all this psychic energy had materialised at one point on his body. All the same, his was an impressive physique. Handed a glass of sherry, the aperitif seemed to disappear into his paw as if already ingested. Invited to sit, the great Grace bottom challenged the joints and glue of the chair.

'My word, am I looking forward to a bite,' he boomed cheerfully.

'You are known as a good trencherman,' Philip responded, with a weak smile. Grace despatched the remark to the boundary without a moment's hesitation.

'You are what you eat,' he agreed.

Bella knew their guest to be a medical man, originally from Bristol; but any tentative pleasantries about the West Country were swiftly brushed aside. The good doctor had come on from Lords, where he had racked up yet another double century with trademark aplomb. It seemed he was perfectly happy to talk about himself with only the minimum of encouragement, while at the same time setting about his meal like a locomotive taking on coal. Even Westland, who had started

9

out like a girl at her first dance, began to wilt under the furnace heat of W. G.'s self-advertisement.

'The secret of the game is in the front foot. There's your boldness, there's your decisiveness. I have played with men who have no more feeling for the front foot than a marble cat,' he rumbled, holding out his plate for a further helping of duck in orange sauce. 'Why, madam, I could teach *you* the off-drive faster than some of the gentlemen who are playing now.'

'And do you think there will one day be women's cricket?' Bella asked.

'I was speaking figuratively, of course,' Dr Grace laughed. 'No, cricket is all boiled beef and carrots or it is nothing. Brawn, in the first instance. It is a village game, played ideally by blacksmiths. I mind Tom Howard, for example, a bull of a man with all the stubbornness of that animal. Sadly gone away into exile.'

'And was his front foot an object of admiration?'

'It was passable,' Grace allowed, swigging from his claret. 'There were faults in it but it was passable.'

The good doctor was beginning to annoy Bella. Her smile was on the thin side.

'As you have discovered,' she said in her best little girl's voice, 'I know very little of the game but I conclude it is one that celebrates the healthy crudities of a male existence.'

'You are in the right of it!' Grace guffawed. This left him open to the unplayable ball, which Bella delivered with some zip.

'And as a consequence perhaps it is beyond a mere woman's understanding.'

The renowned cricketer looked at her under beetling eyebrows. He was, as Mrs Venn might have put it, not quite so green as he was cabbage-looking. Their eyes locked and after a moment he ducked his head with a wry expression.

'You do well to reprove me,' he muttered. 'To speak truthfully, Mrs Wallis, I sometimes bore myself with these stories.'

'My dear Dr Grace, you must not act contrite. You are quite the most famous man I have ever met.'

'I believe not,' the doctor said, blushing. She softened. And the meal ended with Grace's most elegant stroke, which was to beg his hostess to bring the cook to the table that she might receive his thanks. To Bella's utter amazement, Dora Venn might as well have been complimented by the Prince of Wales, so deep were her curtsies.

'I count it an honour, Doctor,' she gushed. 'Why, if my dear departed husband could have been spared to see you here in this room, what a happy man he would be. He used to say to me that barring the talking horse of Shakespeare's day, never was such a prodigy, his exact words.'

'He followed the game?'

'Followed it? He could bore the hind legs off a donkey on the topic.'

Grace laughed and patted her hand with his own bearlike paw.

'Did he see me play?'

'He was the gateman across the river at the Surrey Club. You met him, sir, though you can't hardly be expected to remember. It was Charlie Venn who helped lift the madwoman's curse on you when you first played in London.'

'Now here's a famous story!' Grace exclaimed delightedly.

But if he expected Westland to laugh along with him, he was sorely mistaken. Philip threw down his napkin and turned his face away from Mrs Venn, scowling like a petulant child. The cook looked bewildered.

'I'm sure if I've said anything to upset—' she began hastily—but too late. Philip rounded on her, displaying a lack of manners akin to dragging in a dead cat from the street outside.

'This is mischievous, Dora. Mischievous! I will hear nothing of curses or madwomen, do you understand? Not in this house. Not ever.'

Grace looked perplexed.

'All the same, Westland, the thing did take place. It will cause me no offence at all to hear the story again. And of course it has made not the slightest difference to my batting averages. The contrary, if anything. So much for curses.'

Philip turned to Bella with glittering eyes.

'Are we to endure any more of this?' he barked.

'Let us leave it there, Mrs Venn,' Bella suggested, very alarmed.

'I will not be spoke of like that in front of honoured company,' Dora Venn insisted stubbornly. To everybody's amazement, Philip rose from the table with enough force to tumble his chair.

'And I will hear nothing more of any damn curse,' he shouted. 'Do you understand, all of you?'

There was an appalled silence. Very angry indeed, Bella reached and caught both Mrs Venn's hands in hers. It was a brief enough contact but

12

constituted a complete reproach, though delivered to Philip's back.

After dinner, she did her best to turn the conversation into more general channels, as for example the total number of steamships now in service and whether their activities would have the effect of shrinking the world; the success of Mr Spencer Gore at the All-England tennis final; the course of Russian music, etc. Grace played up to her gallantly but nothing could save the evening. He left a little before half past eleven.

*   *   *

Bella was late to bed. Philip was waiting for her, a book in his hand.

'Bella, believe me, I had no idea what made me say those things,' he mumbled in a sombre voice.

'Mrs Venn is talking of handing in her notice.'

'But that is ridiculous! I shall make my apologies to Dora Venn in the morning. As for Grace, it's in the way of things that we shall never see him again.'

Bella took the book from his hand and threw it at the wall.

'Listen to me. Before this evening I had never heard of W. G. Grace and knew nothing of any curse. We have the great man's assurance that it has done his batting no harm, for which we must be for ever grateful. But you, Philip, are going to have to say more, much more.'

'I cannot.'

'I have never seen you so completely off the rails as you were tonight. We share everything, I believe. We hide nothing. Are you upset about

13

your sister? About Jane? Is that it?'

'I have made it clear before,' he said stiffly, 'that I cannot—will not—speak that name any more, even to you.'

'This is ridiculous. Jane believed—believes—'

'I invited Grace tonight to hear what he has to say about cricket. And—this is the nature of male vanity—because he is famous. Because his fame made me feel important, God help me. Schoolboys think the same way.'

'Did you know about the woman at the Surrey ground before Dora mentioned her?'

Philip's face darkened. He beat with his hands on the counterpane, a muscle jumping in his cheek.

'I was infernally rude to you and Mrs Venn and that is where it must end. I will not be quizzed, Bella. Let it be.'

'You think I have nothing helpful to say on the incident?'

'I think it none of your business.'

Bella flushed. And Philip, seeing that he had wounded her horribly, put his head in his hands. She was amazed to see tears running down his cheeks. She managed to walk out of the room and along to the bathroom without collapsing in dismay. Washed her face, unpinned and brushed her hair for five long minutes, waiting for him to come and find her.

When he did, they kissed and made up. But long after, Bella lay by his side in bed listening to the sleepless city—pub-singing, cries and laughter, and the distant surf of traffic. The night air was sultry and the room smelled stale. She twiddled the edge of the sheet between her thumb and finger.

'Is he so very famous?' she asked, almost to

14

herself. Philip took her hand.

'Grace? As far as cricket goes, he is incomparable. He is still young but already they say there will never be another like him. He is right. If there was a curse, it failed miserably in his case, to be sure.' There was a pause, a long one, and then he said, 'I love you, Bella. No one could love you more.'

In the dark, Bella frowned. An image came into her mind, of a feather falling through air, seemingly weightless but enough to upset the balance of (it was true) some exceptionally sensitive scales. And because she was a novelist, which was to say an intellectual fidget, it was not the quality of the curse that sent her into sleepless discomfort but the identity of the person who had made it.

As only a very few people in London knew, Mrs Bella Wallis was also the sensationalist author Henry Ellis Margam. In Margam's world, the curse was hardly likely to have been laid by a toothless old crone huddled in rags outside the Surrey grounds. A better candidate by far would be some ruined Hungarian noblewoman with connections to vampirism; or an octoroon with violet eyes. Quite what the motive was could only be teased out with further references to haunted houses, bleak moors shrouded in fog, even a ship burning to the waterline in some Arctic landscape.

And none of this helped explain tears at bedtime. Bella sighed. Philip was already asleep at her side, sprawled like a tiler who had fallen through the roof. One of his most enviable gifts was to treat each day as a new day, with the old erased, as surely as the tide destroys a sandcastle.

15

And if it were not like that, to bury the pain so deep that it could never hurt again. In all but a very few things he had succeeded. His sister's madness was an exception.

There was little of imagination in his dreams. The most unintentionally telling was when he was handed a cucumber by the German Crown Princess, who happened to be dressed for skating with a perfectly adorable round fur hat and white kid gloves. The cucumber was, Victoria's favourite daughter explained, the key to eternal happiness. More phlegmatic than his beloved Bella—and twice as innocent—Philip Westland had put the whole thing down to indigestion and a bad pillow.

Bella planted a kiss on his cheek and fell back into a little shaft of moonlight, wanting to think deep thoughts about life and love but caring more for what to say to Dora Venn in the morning.

*   *   *

The following day was bright but blowy. In Fleur de Lys Court, off the Strand, dust devils scurried across the flagstones. Captain Quigley had chosen this unsuitable weather to paint the front door of what Bella thought of as Henry Ellis Margam's office and Quigley described as his occasional summer quarters. The paint came from a little bit of business he had conducted the previous evening at a pub in Bedford Street. A rustic-looking cove (it was the spotted red neckerchief that gave Quigley the idea) was selling the surplus from a job in Long Acre which had concluded that same afternoon.

'So was you on that job?' Quigley asked,

sceptically.

'I was passing by as the ganger was loading his cart,' the rustic cove admitted. 'As a matter of fact, I was going to see my sister-in-law and the opportunity, as you might say, dropped in my lap.'

'You took the paint?'

'I took the cart, mate. Cart and contents. Brisk footwork needed.'

'You thieving rogue,' Quigley said admiringly. 'And this sister-in-law, is she also a countrywoman?'

'Watch it!' the rustic cove warned. 'I ain't no more from the country than you are a peer of the realm, you fat-arse soak.'

'Well, what accent is that?'

Dutch, at one remove. The old father a steward on the Irish ferries, ma a wandering Dutchwoman from Dordrecht. The dodger himself born and brought up in the Smoke.

'This what you see me wearing now, including these here sideburns, is all the rage, matey. We can't all look like Chinese Gordon just before the fuzzie-wuzzies punched his ticket.'

'Point taken,' Quigley agreed, tugging straight his ruined tunic. To smooth over any feelings of ill will, he walked round the corner with the bloke, as the saying goes, and bought a couple of tins of the stolen paint and a good-looking brush or two.

Bella listened to all this while drinking a can of coffee from Tonio's and watching Quigley dab at the door, which he did from a sitting position on a chair that lacked its back.

'And this is why I am now having my front door painted in what appears to be lumpy cocoa,' she commented.

'How did things go with W. G. last night?' Quigley countered nimbly. She gaped.

'And how do you know anything at all about that?'

'It's my business to look after your interests in a general sort of a way. Also, I've had Dora Venn round here screaming blue murder.'

'You look after her general interests, too, do you?'

'Hardly know the woman but I did know Charlie Venn when he was alive. His mother and mine were in service together, over in Russell Square. Charlie a bit on the whimsical side to my taste, as can happen to chapel people. Forever chuckling and rubbing his hands together, if you follow me. Simple, another way of putting it.'

'Or devout,' Bella suggested in her most acid voice.

'Oh, nobody bothered God more regular. No doubt about that.'

'And his part in the lifting of the Oval curse?'

'Ah, the curse!'

'Yes, the curse! Mrs Venn didn't mention it?'

'She spoke of little else. Wondering what had got up Mr Westland's nose so dramatic, him as wasn't even there on the day. Him as calm as a horse pond in the general way of things and about as sporting as a length of staircarpet.'

He laid down the paintbrush without too many regrets and adopted the pose suggesting commanding presence—one leg crossed over the other, a bunched fist tapping the knee from time to time and his free hand set to tugging his nose and stroking his chin. The poet Tennyson had many of the same gestures when in conversation, though in his case they did not lead to a face decorated by unsightly brown smudges.

'We go back ten years,' the Captain began.

TWO

In 1868, the very first party of Australian cricketers came to England to play forty or so matches. Gathered together by a bearded chancer in Sydney, these men had one startling thing in common. They were all of them Aborigines from the Lake Wallace area of Victoria, where they had been taught to play the game by white farmers. When they landed at Gravesend, they were described in a surly piece in *The Times* as 'the conquered natives of a convict colony'. As it happened, there were no convicts in Victoria and the cricketers, though they may have been conquered, were also accomplished stockmen and range riders. To *The Times* readers, as to the rest of England, it hardly mattered who they were, other than representatives of an inferior race, doomed to extinction. Looked at in this light, their presence was an insult to the hallowed game. It did not help their cause at all that they were rather good at playing it.

'Didn't suit,' Quigley explained. 'Perfectly all right as a circus act, say in the manner of footballing dwarves or something along those lines. I don't think you ever met Mad Jack Maloney, but he had rights in a mermaid who was very popular in her day. Tulalula from Tahiti. A homely little body from Battersea Rise. But then, one

19

afternoon—'

'Can we stay with the cricketers?'

'Of course,' Quigley said, magnanimous. 'Ugly coves, most people found them. Black as a cow's insides, cousins to the monkey as regards the face. Big eyes. Sad eyes, as if they were always thinking of something else.'

'And what might that have been?'

'Ho! Perhaps they was musing on something along the philosophical line. Or maybe they was just wondering whether they had left a kangaroo stew on the stove back home.'

This witticism sent him into paroxysms of coughing, which Bella relieved by punching him hard in the back with her clenched fist.

'You met them?' she asked, when the fit was over. The Captain nodded weakly, tears running down his nose.

'The first big match they played was at the Oval. Twenty thousand turned up for the novelty of the thing. Having freely imbibed beforehand. Like I say, me and Charlie Venn were mates and him being the gateman and all, I was privileged to make their acquaintance on a face-to-face basis.'

'You shook their hand and so forth.'

'Better than that. We knocked back a few pints back with Bullocky, Jimmy Mosquito and some others. Yes, quite a few pints at that.'

'This was after the match?'

'Before, during and after. The hand of friendship extended and once extended, gratefully took. Sport knows no boundaries.'

'You mean your impudence knows none.'

'Let me tell you it was a warm day and refreshment much appreciated. By close of play most of the crowd was also in elevated mood, as the poet might put it. At the end of the cricket, the black boys came back out for an exhibition of boomerang throwing. The crowd was raucous, as I say, and for the cricketing purists among us—'

'Get on with it,' Bella snapped.

But the story needed dramatic punctuation and he lit a slightly battered cigar drawn from his tunic pocket.

'There's something about boomerangs,' he explained. 'Very un-English. It got up people's noses. You throw a stick away, you expect it to stay thrown. Anyway, the business over, out come the gentlemen of the Surrey Club and start hurling cricket balls at the black chaps, which they tried to fend off with their traditional shields. All part of the circus atmosphere but it suited the occasion. Old Jimmy Mosquito copped a couple that near enough laid him out. Twopenny caught one on the shins—I can tell you the toffs were not messing about, Mr Margam, sir.'

'These brave men were being deliberately humiliated?'

'That was the idea,' Quigley confirmed. 'The crowd baying and cheering, fat-arse schoolboys in their fifties scampering about, faces red as lobsters. Scenes to shock the faint-hearted.'

'How did it end?'

'The flash mob would have been happy to see the poor savages chased down the Kennington Road with only their boomerangs to cover their shame. I speak figuratively. But then someone came up with the idea of a last competition. Which was: who could chuck a cricket ball the farthest?'

'At which surely the aborigines excelled?'

21

'No one to touch 'em. Prodigious feats accomplished. So now the crowd's gone quiet and more than a bit surly. And for why, we hardly need ask? Tables turned, is for why! The black men is now putting it across the gentry.'

'Good for them!' Bella exclaimed. Quigley chortled.

'Spoken like a bishop. The black boys are chucking for fun when out onto the pitch strolls a portly-looking cove with thighs like a carthorse. Hands like buckets. Twenty years old but could pass for his grandfather. He picks up the pill, which is what we students of the game call it, and bungs it a very casual 118 yards, as measured by the umpires. Pandemonium in the crowd! Jeers of derision for the black coves! The mystery white man has taken 'em down a peg!'

Quigley drew on his cigar with a flourish of which any clubman in London might be proud. He was back in chortling mode.

'Now, dear lady, tell me: Who was this bearded young prodigy? A medical student to be sure. But what was his name?'

It took a moment to sink in.

'Dr Grace beat the aborigines?' Bella asked faintly.

'All ends up. I'll tell you this: they do a lot of magic, these coves, when they're running around the gum trees in Australia. And there, believe me, his name is mud.'

'The native Australians laid the curse?' Bella exclaimed. 'From twelve thousand miles away?'

'No,' the Captain allowed regretfully. 'That came from nearer to home, a witness to this whole sorry scene. To be exact about it, a lady. Much like

22

yourself, Mr Margam. Out of the same box, so to speak. Only difference, she was hanging by the topmost spikes of Charlie Venn's gates and shouting her hat off.'

'A woman laid the curse?'

'A lady,' Quigley corrected. 'One of your lot, as you might say.'

A dreadful possibility occurred to Bella.

'Has any of this to do with Mr Westland or a member of his family?' she asked in a very small voice.

Quigley gawped. Normally, nothing would have pleased him more than to discover black conspiracy at the heart of things, but mention of Philip's name stumped him. He peered at Bella, genuinely perplexed.

'You have lost me, dear lady.'

'What I am asking is, do you know the woman's name?'

'Lady Gollinge.'

Relief flooded Bella. That, and shame at having asked the question.

*   *   *

She walked back to Orange Street in sombre mood. As Quigley pointed out, here was a story begging to be exploited by her writing persona, Henry Ellis Margam. What could be more sensational than a wildly uttered curse and its consequences? The triumphant conclusion Quigley had given to his story pointed like a fingerpost to something that would virtually write itself. And, she thought gloomily, that was it, that was the problem. All she had to do was strip out the aborigines, turn W. G. Grace into the Bishop of Matabeleland, identify the mystery lady as the Countess Paulette D'Ayraud and shift the action from the Oval to the Prix de L'Arc de Triomphe at Longchamps. That was all.

Why stop there? Why not turn Grace into Rupert von Gneisenau and have the lady become Eleanor Atkinson, a tall and willowy blonde who had come across an ancient book of curses in Paris, say in a *bouqiniste*'s bordering the Seine? Begged by her rather scatty mother not to read one aloud, she had done so just as von Gneisenau, a handsome brute of a man, had passed behind her back. Prior to this curse, the young Prussian had been stupidity incarnate. Even the royal house of Prussia, which had great forgivingness when it came to low intelligence, thought him insufferably slow on the uptake. But within months of Eleanor's curse landing on his innocent head, the lights burned at midnight in every Chancellory in Europe. It was war!

There were by now nine Margam books. What had started out as a widow's way of keeping herself busy (which was really to say fending off boredom and despair, not to mention any amount of attention from predatory men) was becoming profitably routine. There was a book going through the press right now, in which bosoms heaved and eyes narrowed, veins pulsed and hair flew in wild disorder. The *mise en scène* of this one was the coast of Pomerania, which was not entirely unlike the country around West Bay, in Dorset.

The public loved Henry Ellis Margam. Her publisher, Elias Frean, admired him, as well he might, for Margam novels comfortably headed the

24

company's sales list. Frean was afraid of Bella, enough to have appointed a man of very different stamp to the London office. This languid fool thought of publishing as a disguised form of self-advertisement: his authors were doing their scribbling to smooth his path to the best salons and the most prestigious dinners. Barely energised enough to light his own cigarettes, certainly too weary of life to finish them, the new director wafted about London, trailing behind him carefully polished offhandedness, first rehearsed to his shaving mirror.

'A good bootmaker is an important fellow. The people who make embroidered waistcoats are quite important and I have heard interesting things said about lighthouse keepers. Authors are like grass, however. As lawns, they make a pleasing background to intelligent conversation.'

This to Bella at their only meeting. It was meant to intimidate her, the way a cruder man might raise a warning stick to an animal. It had a consequence that would have appalled the much more timorous Frean. His principal money-spinner came away from the meeting amused but thoughtful. There was only one response to this ambitious little jackanapes. If she had anything about her she should push Margam under a train and marry Philip Westland. She should do it today.

London was filled with sunshine, but the brisk wind, that in the country would hardly do more than make playful cat's paws in the barley, was here spiteful with grit and dust. The bottom of Charing Cross Road was black with cabs, their canvas roofs jostling each other as they tried to filter into Trafalgar Square. Bella wondered momentarily what all the fuss was about and then blushed for shame. The sculptor Musgrave, whom she knew slightly, was being buried in St Martin's in the Field. The vainglorious old fool Musgrave, with his chaotic private life and long history of sexual disasters. When she was much younger Bella herself had been cornered in his studio with only a broom to save her honour.

The memory did nothing to improve her mood. The air in the streets stank, window glass exploded with the sun's reflections, her feet hurt: it was a classic London summer's day. Like many people who passed her on the crowded pavements, Bella itched to hit someone. Turning into Orange Street, she calmed herself by stopping off at Liddell's and buying a walnut cake she did not need. Old Liddell, who knew a thing or two about human foible, boxed it slowly and carefully without saying a word.

'I will have the boy send it down to you,' he rumbled finally.

'It is hardly worth his trouble. The distance is so short.'

'It will taste better if it is delivered,' Liddell contradicted with a gentle smile.

Soothing encounters like these helped. But then, as Bella approached the house, she was startled to see a small but dapper man leave it, scooting down the steps and hurrying away towards Haymarket. She glimpsed Philip's face at the window for a second. When she came into the drawing room, he was standing in front of the hearth in theatrical pose, his arm along the mantelpiece.

'Where have you been off to this morning?' he

26

asked, far too casually.

'Who was that man who just left the house? And Philip, if you answer, "What man?", which I see you half intend to do, I shall claw at the wallpaper with my fingernails.'

'Your new boots are pinching,' he guessed, entirely correctly.

'His name.'

He hesitated for only a second: Bella had long considered it one of his most lovable characteristics that when cornered he always told the truth.

'He is a naval officer called Alcock. However, it is very important that you forget what I have just said. I mean that, Bella.'

She sat down abruptly, as if all the air had been sucked from the room. Philip shrugged and began to pace about, hands in pocket.

'It had to come out sooner or later,' he muttered to himself, but only when he was behind her and could not see her face. The words were as good as a full confession.

Ever since she had known him, Philip Westland had disappeared three or four times a year on mysterious expeditions, seldom for more than a week yet never once properly explained. A friend had invited him to fish salmon in Perthshire, or an old school acquaintance was dying and destitute in Bath. He was going up to Anglesey to buy a marine picture he never brought home. Much more plausibly, his sister, in the charge of the Jarnac nuns, had taken a turn for the worse.

When she first noticed these absences, Bella supposed he had another woman somewhere, possibly even in London itself. If he did, it was no more than she deserved, for she had refused marriage with him three times and men were apt to misunderstand such matters. But it was not in Philip's nature to divide his affections between two women. Another possibility existed. He had not said and she could not ask but she had begun to believe that he was in the service of the government in some clandestine way.

'May I guess that you are going away for a while?'

'For a few days.'

The misery in his voice was painful to hear.

'Is it dangerous, what you do?'

'Bella,' he implored softly.

'I do not ask where you are going and for what reason; but is it dangerous?'

'No. Of course not.'

She reached into a tortoiseshell box, found a cheroot and lit it with trembling hands. Smoking was a vice he had begged her to give up. He stopped prowling and sat down opposite her, his hands between his knees.

'A week,' he said. 'Maybe ten days. You know all too well I am the least heroic man in London and until now the work has never followed me home here. We are just as we would be if I were a—I don't know, give me an example.'

'A jewel thief.'

'That is unfair.'

Close to an anger she could not explain, she threw her cheroot at the grate and plunged her head in her hands. No words of beseechment from him, no words of any kind. Nothing but the dry cough of the clock.

'Shall you go today?' she asked from between

28

laced fingers.

'Yes,' he said with awful heaviness. 'I don't choose to but I must.'

She jumped up and walked upstairs to the second bedroom. Tore off her new boots and flung them at the wall, before crawling onto the bed fully dressed. She lay on her back, an arm across her face. To calm herself, she tried to remember the name of the sculptor Musgrave's last mistress, a girl he had picked up one night on Battersea Bridge. Flaxen hair, beautifully full lips fashioned into a permanent scowl. Bella had met her only once, walking in Green Park with the hobbling scarecrow that was Musgrave. She hardly spoke a word but the look she gave Bella was unmistakably direct, enough to make the older woman blush. They exchanged complicit glances while the sculptor prattled on about his most recent setback, which was falling off a scaffold in his studio. But her name? Her *name*?

When Westland tiptoed into the room only half an hour later, Bella was fast asleep. He put the note he had written her on the mantelpiece, next to a photograph of them both, she in a high-backed chair with barley-twist pillars, he behind her looking rumpled but content. Even a little smug, as a man might look who had won the great prize of life without really trying too hard.

*   *   *

'Well,' Cissie Comford remarked, helping herself to a third slice of the walnut cake, 'you can have no idea of the dreadful people who attended that funeral. Billy Frith I am sure was drunk; there was

29

a man there who stank of tobacco and turned out to be Carlyle, quite *the* most disagreeable Scotchman in London but Musgrave's Chelsea neighbour; and two hundred others of dubious worth.'

So upset was she that Lady Cornford had gone straight from the service to Harrods (where she always bought her stationery); from there into the Park, where she met such a very nice old man who might well have been Dr Hornby, Provost of Eton; and now here she was on the homeward leg to Bedford Square. It was the arrival of her carriage that wakened Bella. Musgrave's funeral had furnished her with a week's gossip she was anxious to unload. Hornby (if it was Hornby) had endured some of it and now it was Bella's turn.

'Very poor hymns, all of the jocular variety; much prosing from the man who gave the eulogy and an overall lack of elegance. It was said that five of Musgrave's mistresses were represented, either in person or by what I suppose we should call his natural children. Or bastards.'

'And Alice Armstrong? What of her?'

'I can't imagine who you might mean.'

'His last companion.'

'Oh, the Battersea Bundle! She used to work on an asparagus farm, you know, and that's what gave her the soubriquet. Yes, she was there, wearing a veil as big as a tablecloth. We didn't speak, of course.'

'That wasn't very kind.'

'Percy Musgrave was a terrible lecher but his mother had connection to the Cathcart family. There are some unalterable truths, I think, and one of them is that the classes cannot mingle. As

Frith said, rather wittily I thought, a few rows of asparagus can hardly compare with two thousand acres in Norfolk.'

'Frith's father was a pub landlord in Yorkshire,' Bella observed.

'I am sure he was nothing of the sort,' Cissie Cornford declared. She mumbled over her cake for a moment.

'Where is Westland, by the way?' she asked.

'He has gone into the country for a few days.'

'I see. Oh, yes, into the country, is it?'

'I don't suppose that just for once you could try to be a little less knowing,' Bella snapped. Lady Cornford smirked.

'I am sure it is none of my business where he is. How did you get on with Dr Grace? He came to Bedford Square a month or so ago and I declare I found him the most boring man in all Europe.'

'We learned of the curse laid on him in 1868.'

Cissie's cheeks at once coloured with two angry spots. Her thin little lips contracted to a slit.

'What rubbish you do speak sometimes. This is the Oval curse you speak of, is it?'

'I believe Lord Cornford was a Surrey member at the time.'

'He was President. You are so credulous sometimes, Bella. The whole thing was got up as a skit by an impudent young Guards officer. Who was later cashiered, incidentally, for throwing down his sword while on parade.'

'I have been told it was Lady Gollinge who laid the curse.'

'Then you were a fool to believe it,' Cissie snapped. 'Oh, I daresay Ursula Gollinge said as much at the time but she was quite mad. Her poor

31

husband was in a strait-jacket in Weybridge and she was if anything in worse condition. No house in London would receive them.'

'How was this?'

'Gollinge was something to do with government in Melbourne. Booted out, of course. Quite the wrong type, although one can never know at the outset. She, however, was lunatic from the cradle. It was in the family. Irish, of course.'

'Perhaps she was merely eccentric,' Bella suggested.

'When in Australia, she ran off with a German— a *German*, if you will—to explore the interior. I suppose that counts as mere eccentricity to you. Gone three months and found stark naked and babbling. Stark *naked*. Of the German, no sign. That did for Gollinge. He was invited to resign his post.'

Cissie Cornford had a generally good opinion of Bella but once in a while she closed her face against her. This was such a moment. She wiped her lips with her napkin and then threw it to the carpet.

'It is usual in such situations to draw a veil over events. We do not speak of such persons. I thought you might understand that.'

'Is she still alive?'

'I do not know and do not wish to know. I have explained: it was that scamp Harry Bagot who got up the idea of a curse. *His* family knew how to behave. A week after throwing down his sword in such an exhibition of petulance, the young man was sent to Canada. We shall not be hearing from him again.'

'The silence has closed over him,' Bella

32

murmured.

'Yes, indeed! And what else, pray? I declare, you sometimes talk like one of those infernal novelists.'

Cissie indicated with a brusque gesture that she wished to be pulled up from her chair.

'Some things are regrettable and some contemptible. I hope I shall go to my grave knowing the difference. You don't have servants, I recall, so perhaps you will help me to my carriage. I am very disappointed in you, Bella.'

Are you, you foolish old woman? Bella thought, steering her down the steps to her carriage. But Cissie, as so often happened as she grew older, overplayed her hand.

'I am sure Westland would understand. His mother was an Egerton.'

'He speaks of little else,' Bella assured her. 'We have a cannon on the roof that we let off in honour of that noble lady's birthday.'

And was rewarded by Cissie's peering upward glance to see whether this might just be true. It was only when walking back into the house that Bella remembered she could not tweak Philip's nose and ask whether he knew anyone called Gollinge. He was, she supposed, being sick on the Dover Ferry.

THREE

Bella sat with a pen in her hand, her face screwed up like a woman who had barked her shin against a chair, or found one favourite earring but not the other. It was half past four in the morning. Waking to find herself alone in the bed, she had dragged

33

herself to a small writing table and a likewise empty sheet of paper, unless one counted the ink stars with which she peppered it. For something to do, she forged her lover's signature, feeling very baleful about it too.

What was a spy? A foreigner, was Henry Ellis Margam's predictable answer. A low fellow; failing that, a gentleman who was traitor to his class. Dr Johnson's scoundrel. The shadowy sort who is always on the outside looking in, never on the inside looking out. A cad. It was these and other such sniggerings that woke Bella from her sleep.

The ideal Margam spy hung about the champagne bar at British Embassy balls in Paris or Vienna. Masked by a black silk scarf, he rode like the wind down moonlit valleys towards some mountaintop schloss. Or then again (uncomfortable thought) he was illuminated by candlelight in a Hungarian spa hotel while his dupe, the foolish virgin with the palest and plumpest of white shoulders, cowered in the corner of the room, having tried to escape and found the door locked. The sheets on the bed were rumpled.

A spy must have at least one scar. He must be a crack shot with a grudge against all humanity. The cruelty of his lips would put a wolf to shame. There must be something additionally unspeakable about him, a secret lust that tickles the reader into guilty speculation as the chapter ends.

Philip Westland had none of a spy's attributes. He was as English as Cheddar cheese, could not ride, shoot or defend himself with his fists. He was, she judged spitefully, at least two stone overweight, prone to bumping into furniture and laughing immoderately at his own clumsiness. He was

34

certainly a wizard at looking up train timetables and retrieving interesting trivia from the pages of *The Times*, as for example the capital of Peru, or Abraham Lincoln's birthplace. But remembering to say he loved her, commending her choice of hats or shoes, finding pleasure in her skin or eyes, was beyond him. 'Everything about you is perfect,' he protested when she chided him for a want of compliments.

He could peel an apple with one continuous (though painstaking) passage of a knife. Seas— boisterous lakes, even—made him feel sick. Beautiful women tied his tongue; and as for dancing, there were bears all over southern Europe who could do as well, or better. At balls or soirées, he stood about grinning like an ape. He had only the one scar—a silvery crescent on his hip, got by tobogganing downstairs on a tea tray when he was eight.

He spoke excellent French and German and had tourist Italian. Without Bella in the world he would have gone to India three years earlier and added Hindi to the list. He might even be married. Or, as Margam warned in her ear, he might be chained to the wall in some Afghani fortress, or dead in a ditch outside the Poona cantonments. But of one thing she was certain. Without her he would have remained loveless. Without *him*, she told her alter ego, Henry Ellis Margam, I might have died of crabbiness and boredom. Tears dropped onto her cheeks and ran towards her chin.

There was a rumble of iron rims in the street outside. The greengrocer was back from Covent Garden with a few boxes and crates of fresh vegetables. During his absence his boy had opened up the shop and swept the pavement. Together they began unloading the produce, talking to each other in low voices, like conspirators at the opera.

Bella shucked off her nightgown and lay down on the bed, letting the breeze from the open window cool her naked back. The curse laid on the ox-like Dr Grace caused him much less disquiet than the misery she felt now.

*   *   *

At breakfast there was a five-week-old letter with an American postmark. The wonderfully guileless Mary Kennett, so recently married to Philip's great friend, William, was writing from Denver at the end of a six-month honeymoon. By the greatest of good fortune, they had come across a gentleman from California who had sold them a map of some gold-bearing reefs in his part of the world that were hitherto unexplored. Now nothing must do but to make their way there as soon as possible— and under conditions of complete secrecy. The map was a little vague, for something that cost so much to purchase, but William had invented an improved separator that she felt well able to operate while he dug out the banks of the river along which the gold was located. Campfires and— a classic Mary touch—skylarks were indicated.

Yesterday Wm entered a shooting competition with the local gentry, if such they can be described. More accurately, he was given a pistol and invited to take aim at an empty whiskey bottle flung into a nearby creek. You well know his ignorance of firearms but at his

36

first shot he removed the neck (at a range of forty paces) adding with the greatest offhandedness that he considered the body of the bottle too easy a target. A very large man with a red beard then accused him of a lucky chance, saying he had his eyes tight shut when he fired. Why, said Wm, he had no idea the rules were otherwise and gave back the pistol, saying he was d—d if he was going to be put upon for acting the way any English sportsman would, faced with such an easy task etc., etc. You are the dangfool dude who bought the gold map, Mr Redbeard countered, amid much laughter. That was a lucky chance, what you just did with the bottle. See and if you can shoot me, who is stood here right before you! So Wm took back the pistol and shot the man very satisfactorily, the bullet passing through his boot, to much ribaldry.

We take train to California tomorrow, in company with a dog sold to us earlier, one who it is claimed has an infallible nose for gold (tho I wd say he has been brought out from retirement for this present expedition, his nose likely to be his last fully functioning organ, for the poor fellow can hardly walk and barks only if you tread upon him).

Wd you please give Mr Murch an account of the shooting contest, for it is Wm's great regret that he was not here to witness it. Finally, dearest Bella, to you my deepest, deepest love, Mary. P.S. We have called the dog Quigley.

Mrs Venn observed the envelope and its frank with great contentment when she came in to clear the table, for the Kennetts were her favourites among Bella's friends, Mary especially. Her mood was sunny. Before he left so suddenly, Philip had gone down into the kitchen and made up with Dora, begging her forgiveness and going so far as to kiss her cheek. A few words now about his dearest pal in life would happily restore things to easy normality.

'How lucky that young man is to have found such a soulmate and that's no error. A prettier creature never was. And him such a Mr Head-in-the-Clouds for the most part.'

'He is prospecting for gold now, Mrs Venn,' Bella smiled.

'Hmmph,' Dora Venn snorted. 'Well, I hope he has bought his wife a sizeable hat and veil for it would be a crime to see her come home with that lovely complexion of hers ruined. Foreign parts indeed! Same as I said to Mr Westland—'

Her voice stopped in its tracks and she blushed guiltily. When she looked up she found Bella's gaze very level indeed—the notion of icy daggers occurred to her as a fancy.

'What did you say to Mr Westland?'

'Well, I shall not beat about the bush, though it costs me my position. I told him I thought it ripe that he should gad about all on his ownio over there, leaving you behind to wring your hands like a sailor's wife. Not that I say you do,' she added hastily, 'and not that the two of you are married.'

'You mentioned "over there".'

'France, is it? The way I see it, Mrs Wallis—and I've said too much to turn back now—we should leave these Frenchies and all the rest of them to stew in their own juice. Venn, when he was alive,

38

was very hot on the subject. All the wailing and gnashing of teeth that goes on.'

'I have not heard that mentioned before in connection with Europe.'

'The Pope,' Mrs Venn explained. 'He encourages it. Just across from us in Coleman Street, when we lived on that side of the river, bless me if we didn't have half of Italy yelling and banging and cutting up on a Saturday night. Nice enough creatures but I couldn't help but think they'd be better off at home among their own. I used to say to Mrs Tubney—'

'Who sounds comfortingly English—'

'None more so. Well, indeed, her boy Arthur went across the river to be a constable with the police. I don't know as how you can get more respectable than that. Not from where we came from.'

'Do you ever see him, this Arthur?' Bella asked in a lazy sort of way, to indicate that she could hardly be bothered with the reply. She was imagining some chance encounter at a road crossing with a moustachioed giant. What Mrs Venn said next brought her bolt upright in her chair.

'He was the one that arrested Lady Gollinge for her wild words in that matter we was discussing two nights ago, to do with Dr Grace.'

'Mrs Tubney's son?'

'As I live and die. It was his first pinch.'

'Where can I find him? Do you know what division he is in?'

'I do not. I thought we was discussing the Pope.'

But Bella was reacting mostly to the previous day's acid conversation with Cissie Cornford. From

39

being a story she could take or leave alone, a certain pride (and a good measure of exasperation) made it important to track down this curse and its author. She would not be put upon as nothing but a mere scribbler. Or woman, she added for Westland's discomfort, hoping to make his ears burn in whatever foreign bedroom he was taking off his trousers with trademark modesty.

* * *

Quigley vaguely remembered the bloke who laid his hand on Lady Gollinge's collar, though ten years had effaced the detail. And no, he did not propose to walk up to the nearest copper on the street and put the question about his present whereabouts. It was his experience of the Met that if you showed interest in them they were often of a mind to show a greater interest in you. This was a job demanding the calling in of favours from among those who were, as you might say, the best clients of the police—fellow professionals, so to speak. A good thief or burglar, if he had anything about him at all, could furnish a complete biography of the police force, down to what they had for breakfast. Why, hadn't he seen that very morning Topper Lawson sloping away down the Strand, a walking encyclopedia of rooftop London with broad experience of the Old Bill and its organisational structure?

'I do not wish to stir a hornet's nest,' Bella cautioned.

'Ho! As to that, no more do I. A few quiet words in the right ear, say towards lunchtime when the pubs have warmed up. Topper Lawson our man.

Bald as an egg but a mighty brain beating there. Knows everybody. An ace up his sleeve for all occasions.'

'Can he be found easily?'

'He is the weather in the streets,' Captain Quigley explained. 'Meaning he is everywhere. As for the quality of his information, does a good bun have a cherry on the top?'

*   *   *

Under other circumstances, Bella might have taken advantage of Quigley's departure to do a little work on her next novel, for Margam worked strict office hours and liked to keep busy, as he put it. A chance conversation with a charismatic vicar from Norfolk a week or so ago had given him the germ of an idea. Big beaches clouded in spume, a girl's corpse rolling in the lap of the tide and the vicar, the great fool, sobbing like a baby on the altar rail of some forsaken village church. Up in the great house, General MacAlhone has dressed himself in his ancient blues, the better to blow his brains out in a final act of gallantry.

Quigley, with his unerring sense of what was in the air, had laid out her best German nibs and favourite ivory penholder. He had even gone so far as to tear a page from a child's atlas of Great Britain that indicated a broad sweep of the Norfolk coast. All to encourage a bout of wordsmithery, his expression for it. It kept the lady cheerful. Or if not that, occupied. Mr Westland gadding about, as per. Naturally, the dear woman turns to her scribbling.

'Blind me if you ain't nothing but a wicked old gossip, Captain,' Hannah Bardsoe grumbled, half a

41

mile from Fleur de Lys Court. 'Never you mind what she does or doesn't choose to do with her time. You as can barely write your own name.'

'Now who's being wicked?'

'She gave you a little commission this morning and you ain't going to get far with it sitting here in my parlour, drinking my rum and preening yourself.'

'Bear in mind I am carrying the heavy end of the wardrobe nowadays. I don't see the old gang gathering round, as used to be. You and Charlie tucked up here in Shelton Street like Hansel and Gretel. Mr Kennett wandering about America. And as for Billy Murch, I have seen neither hide nor hair of him these past three months.'

'And I wonder why?' Hannah asked cuttingly. 'You got to get this gang business out of your hair, Percy Quigley. The lady is an author. She don't want to be forever messing with the sort of rubbish that fills your head.'

'Oh, well, thanks very much for that,' he said, injured. 'Give old Perce a kicking, why don't you? I have done that woman a few favours in the past, my oath if I haven't.'

'Yes, you have. But suppose it is all over? Suppose she marries Mr Westland as by rights she should, the poor man? If he has a mind to marry her, that is.'

'Nothing more certain.'

'Well, there you are, then. Any old how, what is this thing she's asked you do for her this morning?'

When he told her, Hannah's face fell.

'That ain't right,' she said. 'Nothing but harm can come from asking after the police. They take that sort of thing very bad, the jumped-up busybodies. Oh, this is very bad! Stop her, Perce. Don't let her go down that road. What's his name again, this cove?'

At that moment Bella was walking home to Orange Street, leaving the fictional General MacAlhone examining the handwriting on certain envelopes and wondering what the blazes was happening to him, a hero of Talavera. One minute he was being brought to life, cork leg, smallpox scars and all—and the next, pfft. Back in the goddamn desk drawer. My heart is not in it, Bella explained guiltily.

She passed two policemen along the way home, either of whom could have been Arthur Tubney. Her favoured candidate was a big-bellied constable carrying a lost child (or possibly an apple thief), his brawny forearm under her naked rump, her legs dangling like dirty paper streamers.

'Don't you listen to him, darling!' a wit yelled. 'He ain't got no 'ouseboat on the Thames, nor no doggie called Rufus neither.'

'You shut your mouth,' the child piped. 'He's giving me a lift up Long Acre is what he's doing.'

'That's how it starts, girl! Ask your ma, she'll tell you!'

*   *   *

Sergeant Tubney presented himself at Orange Street that afternoon. Bella was astonished on several counts. She had not expected him to come to her, nor was she prepared for how he looked. Tubney was only a little above medium height but what he lacked in inches he made up for in the basilisk calm of his expression. He wore plain

43

clothes—a blue-black worsted suit and discreetly embroidered waistcoat. He wore his hair oiled and brushed straight back. His stock was tied to perfection. All this Bella found faintly intimidating.

'You are a *detective* sergeant perhaps, Mr Tubney?' she guessed.

'I have been with the detective branch four years. In April we became what we call the Criminal Investigation Department.'

'An elite force!'

'A specialist department of the service,' Tubney corrected. The eyes were dark, almost black. The accent was unmistakably a London one; but, as to tone, neutral. In Bella's fictions, policemen were as awkward and clumsy as dogs when they were in the drawing room. This one had a stockbroker's poise.

'You wished to see me, I understand?' he prompted.

'I am first trying to recover from astonishment that you came to the house,' Bella countered. Tubney inclined his head.

'I have taken a small liberty in calling on you, that is true. I was on my way back to the office. To Scotland Yard, if you prefer.' The detective smoothed the fabric of his trousers over his knee. His self-possession was alarming, as was his next remark.

'I have read your books with some interest, Mrs Wallis,' he observed.

'Books? What books? I have written no books. You have been misinformed.'

Tubney said nothing but merely stared at her. The clock ticked. Bella chewed her lip.

'Very well. I wonder how you knew that?' she

capitulated. 'It is a secret I have shared with very few people.'

'I understand. To reassure you, perhaps, the police are good at keeping secrets, when they have to.'

'What else do you know about me?' Bella asked.

'All that is for another time,' Tubney said offhandedly, as though there did indeed exist a bulging dossier somewhere on a windowsill in Scotland Yard. 'But on this occasion I think *you* wanted to ask *me* a question or two. If it would lighten the mood a little, I could say that it was a chance to meet Dora Venn again that brought me here. She was very good to me when I was a nipper.'

Maybe, Bella thought swiftly, but how did you know she was my housekeeper? A warning rocket went off in her head. Tubney, though he realised he had made a slip, watched her impassively, his hands on his knees, shoulders square to the back of the sofa. An unpleasant and faintly ridiculous idea occurred to her: Had her relationship with Philip Westland put the house under surveillance? Is this what happened to spies before they were recruited? That their personal dealings were investigated by the police at the behest of some shadowy government office, say in a memo scribbled by Commander Alcock, RN? She made a huge effort to put these thoughts to one side.

'Mrs Venn told me recently about your very first arrest and I was intrigued enough to hunt you down, as it were. That is all.'

Some of Tubney's aplomb deserted him. He looked genuinely puzzled.

'This is unexpected,' he said.

45

'In what way? You mean, you thought some other topic might be raised?'

The silence that followed suggested that was indeed what he thought he was there for. The two studied each other like cats on the same garden wall. Could it really be that this Tubney, with all his slightly sinister suavity, was gatekeeper to the world into which Philip Westland plunged from time to time?

'Do you happen to know a Commander Alcock, RN?' she asked, feeling heated and reckless (and silently asking forgiveness of Philip Westland). Just like a cat's, Tubney's blink was no more than a washing of the eyeballs.

'It hardly seems likely, does it?'

Mrs Venn came in with the tea. The detective smiled.

'Hullo, Dora,' he murmured.

'Well, here's a turn-up! Little Artie! And you looking so prosperous and all. So the police didn't suit you after all, eh? What line of work are you in now, you clever boy?'

'Mr Tubney is a detective sergeant, Mrs Venn,' Bella supplied. 'He has risen in the world somewhat.'

'Well, I'm blowed! Sergeant, you say? They don't hand those out every day of the week, I am sure.'

'Just leave the tray if you will, Dora,' Tubney said calmly. And even Dora Venn could see that it was not his place to order her about, sergeant or no bloody sergeant. She flushed.

'Yes,' she said. 'Now I remember you all right. They haven't learned you no new manners, I see. My mistress is Mrs Wallis here and not you, you bag of wind.'

And with that she clumped out, heartening Bella incredibly. She seized the moment, busying herself with the teacups.

'It's all very simple, Mr Tubney. At the outset of your career you arrested Lady Ursula Gollinge on a charge of—what was it?—a breach of the peace? To refresh your memory, the arrest took place at the Surrey Cricket Ground. The lady in question was hanging from the decorative gates.'

'She was only later identified as Lady Gollinge. I cautioned her and she struck me in the face with her fist. In such an instance, it was my duty to arrest her. For what it is worth, I was later commended by Assistant Commissioner Havelock for my conduct.'

'Wasn't that very unusual?'

'I had been mentioned favourably by name in a memorandum prepared by members of the Surrey Cricket Club. The situation was far from simple and straightforward, as I believe you already know.'

'Because of the curse?'

Tubney shrugged. It was a careless and even contemptuous gesture, meant to indicate she was asking the wrong question: What mattered was a youthful constable's sense of duty. He had arrested someone from a class that was not usually seized by the waist and dragged to the ground in a public place. The matter was hardly likely to be understood by what Tubney and his colleagues often referred to as civilians.

'It is the curse that interests me,' Bella pressed.

'Some wild words were uttered. Calling down woe on the Surrey Cricket Club, Mr Gladstone,

47

and others.'

'Dr Grace, as he is now?'

'Dr Grace, the Archbishop of Canterbury and, unfortunately, Her Majesty.'

'These were wild words indeed. Did she have anything to say about you?'

Tubney hid his thumb inside his palm. His face darkened. He could remember in the most exact detail sitting on the lady's stomach and having her screech, 'This officer is touching my breasts! He is making a sexual assault! Is that what you came to see, you swine?' As he scrambled clear of her she kicked him in the groin, a pain that resembled being stabbed by an icicle. The crowd cheered.

'Most people assumed she was drunk,' he muttered.

'Was she charged as such?'

'For assaulting a police officer in the course of his duties. She was bailed to appear before magistrates a week hence.'

'And you never saw her again. Nobody saw her again. She never came to court for what she said and did.'

Tubney hesitated. She realised with sudden intuition that his value to the police was not an investigative mind at all, but merely a certain manner. And, just like any actor fed the wrong line, he could be knocked off his stride. She handed him his tea and then reached for the tortoiseshell box on the table between them and selected and lit a cheroot, without offering him one. Very satisfyingly, Tubney's sense of what was expected of a gentlewoman at four o'clock in the afternoon was offended. His cheeks reddened.

'May I pour you some tea, Mrs Wallis?'

48

'I shall do that for myself when I am ready. Do they smoke at Scotland Yard, I wonder? I should imagine it is like Euston station at certain times of the day. But you were saying, Detective?'

'Lady Gollinge had the protection of her class and sex,' Tubney grumbled. 'She was also to be pitied. Her mind was deranged. I do not know what happened to her or where she went after she broke the conditions of her bail.'

'But of course you do! You were then a very junior police constable. But you are something rather grander now. You know exactly where she is, I am sure.'

'I cannot discuss police matters,' he said, much too stiffly.

'Isn't that rather lame? If this had ever been a proper police matter, she would have been found and brought to justice long ago. Instead, one can imagine a Treasury solicitor advising her ladyship to quit London if she had any sense left. And she took that advice and skipped, isn't that it? You got a punch on the nose for your troubles and a letter of commendation from Sir Edward Havelock. She got the liberty to rant and curse in some other part of the kingdom.'

'Why does any of this interest you?'

She thought about that. Nothing in what Tubney had revealed about the Oval incident could possibly have to do with Philip Westland. As Quigley said, he was not in the slightest bit sporty (apart from an accidental skill with archery) and—as far as Bella could remember—had never once expressed an interest in cricket, up to the time a club friend had taken him to Lords to see Grace face his first ball of the second innings, or some

49

such nonsense. Nor had he ever mentioned Lady Ursula Gollinge. A further thought occurred to her. To curse a man like Westland would be like throwing the contents of a cup of tea at the face of Mont Blanc. He was not made for curses.

Which left her with the violence of his reaction when the subject had arisen at the dinner table two nights ago.

'I intend to visit Lady Gollinge,' Bella said in her most offhand tone. 'I will not trouble you for the address for I can get that from Sir Edward, I am sure.'

'You know Sir Edward?' he almost yelped.

'Isn't that something a good detective would already have discovered? Fie on you, Mr Tubney. I do believe you came here to intimidate me in some way. That was very reckless of you. You do not say for certain whether you do or you don't know Commander Alcock. That is, of course, also something I shall take up with him personally. What an interesting and entertaining hour of your time you have given me.'

She rose to indicate that he could put down his cup and leave, thinking guiltily at the same time that Philip Westland, wherever he was, must be wondering from whence the sudden griping pain in his guts had come.

* * *

The bit that alarmed Captain Quigley most was how the police had come to learn of Bella's other self, the scribbler Henry Ellis Margam.

'There's something naughty in that, dear lady, something very naughty. There are things in those

50

books that come a bit close to home. They might be harmless tales to the innocent but raise a few questions to them as can put two and two together.'

'What do you have in mind?'

'What do I have in mind? One or two dead bodies is what I have in mind, one or two unexplained visits to meet the Maker. I don't like it. The Met can be a very nosy neighbour.'

She thought as much herself but had begun to wonder whether it was the police who took the interest or merely the pushy and ambitious Sergeant Tubney.

'You need not trouble yourself. I am going away into the country for a few days.'

'Ho! *You're* going away, are you? Well, let me tell you, Captain Quigley is also pressed to leave London by urgent business in, say, Portsmouth. I don't say he's got our number entirely, this here Tubney, but it don't look good. So we shall lock up here tonight.'

'I shall need to warn Mr Murch.'

'That's it—warn all our mates—Mr Urmiston and Billy Murch—and bunk off out of it for a while. Muy pronto, as they say in France.'

'You think we are being watched?'

'I'm not stopping to find out. I don't know where you're going—'

'Yorkshire,' Bella supplied.

'Well,' Quigley exclaimed in admiration. 'Now that *is* a stroke and no error.'

Yorkshire, Finland, Greenland's icy mountains, they were all the same in the Captain's mental geography—places a long way off and peopled by self-absorbed coves who would not know the

Metropolitan police from the Metropolitan Water Board. Vikings, many of them. Those that weren't, short arses with teeth like piano keys. He wished *he'd* thought of Yorkshire.

'I must go across to Chiswick and warn Mr Murch,' Bella said.

'Want me to do it?'

'No. I'll do it.'

She was making the tedious and expensive journey to warn Billy, to be sure, but also to draw comfort from his imperturbable common sense. Quigley seemed to understand this in his habitually jealous way. He scrubbed his head with his knuckles. Was going to say something but his stock of facetiousness had deserted him. They both started up suddenly like criminals at the sound of a footfall outside. But it was only a gentleman who had ducked into the Court to relieve himself before moving on up the Strand.

FOUR

Billy Murch was as grave and attentive as anyone could wish. Living in William Kennett's Chiswick house as its caretaker had tidied him up, so that he no longer had the look of a man who would as soon sleep out on the lawn as anywhere else. Some of this new gravitas came from his marriage to Millie Rogerson, Kennett's housekeeper. Millie liked her man to walk her to church of a Sunday and while she was careful not to badger him too much about clothes and razors, some of her own haphazard sense of propriety had rubbed off. True, to anyone who had ever drunk a pint in a pub he was still a dangerous-looking cove, lean and lithe with the fighter's knack of watchful stillness. Yet something very good had come to him since marrying. He and his new wife were—or so it seemed to Bella—the poster advertisement of a contented couple. She was thunderingly jealous and said as much.

'I don't know that jealousy's just the right word,' Billy smiled. 'But Millie—and Mr Kennett's library—have helped me turn a corner and that's true enough.'

'This is certainly a house of books. What are you reading at present?'

'Did you know about the Ice Ages, both big and little? There's a lot to chew on there. Though the greater education has come from Millie, of course.'

'Indeed. And I couldn't help noticing—'

'Yes,' he murmured shyly. 'She'll no doubt tell you about it when she comes back. She has gone to sit with her friend, who is in like condition.'

'My heartiest congratulations, Billy. I know Mr Westland will be delighted to hear the news when he returns from the Continent.'

She watched him closely. Murch merely nodded. Perhaps Philip abroad on the Continent was just that to him, an unimportant social note, a thing of no great consequence. Well, of course it was, she reasoned giddily. If Murch was party to this spying business, he would be shoulder to shoulder with Philip right now, primed pistols in his luggage. No better man in a tight corner, no more ruthless an opponent of wrong in the world. If she thought he would do it, Bella would gladly have paid Billy Murch to look after the wandering light that

53

was her soulmate. Which uncomfortable thought brought her back to the reason for her visit.

They started out in the kitchen but at her suggestion moved into Kennett's sitting room, where most of the furniture was shrouded in dust-sheets. Without being asked, Murch lit a small fire in the grate, for while there was ample light left in the sky, the room smelled faintly of damp. So they sat, practically knee to knee, surrounded by icebergs.

Billy listened to her account of Sergeant Tubney's visit to Orange Street with his usual unblinking calm. When she mentioned Quigley's recruitment of Topper Lawson to locate the detective sergeant, he permitted himself a short and wintry smile. Otherwise he heard her out in silence. When she finished her report, he sat looking at his hands for a moment or two. Bella waited.

'We can start with Topper Lawson,' he said. 'There is no bigger cockroach in all London. I don't know what Perce Quigley thought he was doing messing with him. I have had my run-ins with that man before now, you understand. A sack of mischief from Shoreditch you wouldn't trust to point out Nelson's Column, not if you was stood in Trafalgar Square at the time.'

'Quigley described him otherwise.'

'Perce is very easily taken in,' was Billy's terse comment. 'It's my guess that Lawson gabbed to this Tubney cove, making up as much as he dared—and for why? Because he is a well-known copper's nark is for why.'

'He gabbed?'

'Told what he knew, or thought he knew. Which

54

was nothing very much. See—forgive me, Mrs Wallis, if I speak frankly now—you might want to keep your book-writing a secret from the circle that you move in and all power to you for that. But I have to tell you, I knew Henry Ellis Margam was a woman long before I met you.'

'Quigley!' Bella snorted.

'No,' Billy corrected gently. 'It was a bargee's wife who told me, a Gravesend chum of mine with a taste for literature, as you might say.'

'And how did she know about it?'

Murch shrugged. 'How does anyone find out anything? Same as I am walking along Strand on the Green last week and an old bloke with a beard sticks his head out the pub window and shouts, "Looking forward to being a dad, then? Her brains and your beauty, what?" My hand to God, I had never seen this cove before in my life.'

'What did you do?'

'I had him out in the yard and we exchanged a few words, more for the form of the thing than anything else. An ex-Marine, he was. How he knew me was a mystery.'

'I think you're trying to be kind to me, Billy.'

'Not a bit of it. Think of it this way. Somebody says something to Topper Lawson. Could be anybody, could have been last week, last month, or years back. Well, now—begging your pardon once again—who cares? Among our sort of people, who gives so much as a monkey's if you are this Margam bloke? It don't alter the price of fish, as Millie would say. But then along comes Perce, the great chump, and Topper sees his chance to grass you up.'

'Me, or all of us. Quigley thinks that if the

Margam books are read in the right way, they offer clues to—well, let's say certain real-life events. You're not afraid of what might be uncovered?'

Billy looked at her very levelly indeed.

'I don't believe I am,' he said.

'You don't think the police might put two and two together?'

'I've seen them try once or twice,' Billy said drily.

Impulsively, Bella jumped up and kissed him on the cheek. He blushed and fumbled for a cheroot.

'The Tubneys of this world are ten a penny,' he muttered. 'And it's my experience that the only use the law has for a long arm is to find its arse. Put it all behind you, Mrs Wallis. I don't say how, but you can count on it going away. You say you have a mind to visit Yorkshire?'

'I need not go if I can be of help here.'

Billy smiled and smoothed back a glossy wing of hair.

'Nobly put, but I think I shall manage,' he declared, with just enough spin on the words to make Bella blush in turn.

'I feel guilty at having brought all this down on us,' she said.

'We have seen our way through worst scrapes. But on this one, you have been putting the terrier down the wrong rabbit hole, believe me. And now if I don't hear Millie and her bump banging about in the kitchen. I wonder at me saying these words but can I press you to a cup of cocoa, Mrs Wallis?'

*　　　*　　　*

Try as she might, Bella was a timid traveller. She

56

arrived early at train stations, checked platform numbers and departure boards far too casually in an effort to appear nonchalant—and then worried she was on the wrong train, had mislaid her ticket, packed unsuitable clothes, was sitting with people who could not possibly be going where she wanted to go. The answer was to take some improving book and bury oneself in it at once. (Hers was on the hall table in Orange Street, where she had left it.) Someone once told her—it was the gloomily lubricious Musgrave, now departed this earth— that in the early days of train travel it was medical opinion that any speed exceeding forty miles an hour would displace women's internal organs. Their wombs would collapse. She was thinking about this ancient nonsense when the platform guard's whistle shrieked immediately outside the carriage window. It was very annoying to be seen to flinch.

As the train pulled out from King's Cross, it ran for a mile or so through sooty canyons but then the sun burst through the haze and smoke and revealed the tenderest landscapes of brick and tile, where people who would never pass Bella's windows in Orange Street sauntered about streets she too would never visit. Within another hour the view from the carriage was all green, green, green. What seemed to be untenanted countryside stretched and yawned all the way to the horizon. A church tower was an event; two naked boys up to their hips in a willow-lined stream were as startling as a visitation by angels.

She travelled dressed in a bulky tweed suit and yellow boots, topped by an unfortunate quasi-military cap, a sort of purple kepi. Though she was quite resigned to looking four parts out of five a complete idiot in this modest disguise, it served well, for she spent a genial hour exchanging pleasantries about perambulation with a parson from Sittingbourne who was on his way to walk from Lincoln Cathedral back to Canterbury, via Ely and Norwich. So detailed was his itinerary that when he left the train at Grantham, she was perfectly able to pass this off as one of her own former accomplishments to the man who took his seat.

'You are fond of walking,' Mr Buttersby of Sheffield observed.

'It stimulates the circulatory system and the historical imagination in about equal measure,' Bella explained, quoting her parson.

'Does it?' Buttersby muttered. 'Well, there's many as walk the roads of this country in hope of a crust of bread and nothing more. Who keep moving for fear of the workhouse and to escape the cruel necessities of wage slavery.'

'You are a social philosopher,' Bella suggested.

'I am a cattle auctioneer, madam,' he corrected sourly.

After which, he folded his hands over an aldermanic belly and slept.

Bella played with her gloves and thought about Tubney and spies and madwomen, all without any useful conclusion. There *was* one obstinate and indigestible truth in her reflections, which was that she was making this journey, at any rate in part, to spite Philip Westland. Maybe there was a better way of phrasing it but if he could forgo the comforts of Orange Street (among which she counted a tangle of limbs in a crowded bed) then

58

so could she.

Furthermore, this solitary expedition was a way of reasserting her professional independence. Let Philip go about the Continent, peering out of carriage windows and making notes on his cuff, hiding messages in loaves of bread (or whatever else spies did): she too had mysteries and enigmas. The previous evening, Captain Quigley had infuriated her by suggesting that he had better come with her to Yorkshire to keep an eye on things, as he put it. Her sudden flare of anger startled him.

'I was only thinking of your safety, dear lady,' he protested.

'And does every woman who travels alone require the services of a dishevelled drunk?'

'A military mind trained in the arts of reconnaissance is what you meant to say. At any rate, a man, d'you see? For when things get uppity. As you can rest assured they will.'

'And what makes you think that?'

' "Why, I should say you was the very lightning rod to evil," ' he quoted from a sentence she wished she had never written in *Captain Jeffrey's Downfall*. 'I should never forgive myself if you came to grief, never again hold my head up high to such as Mr Westland.'

'I am hardly going to the ends of the earth,' she countered weakly. 'And you can leave Mr Westland out of it.'

'Better you tell him that,' he grunted, always the man to have the last word.

Leeds was just such a town that might have been invented by Quigley for the general disparagement of those unlucky enough not to have been born in

London. Bella arrived just when the day shifts were walking out of the Hunslet factory gates like an exhausted army, heads down, cloth capped, dogged. The tobacco-brown smoke of what looked like a great battle drifted eastwards over the rooftops. In Boar Lane it was difficult to see the road surface for a bickering concourse of horse-drawn buses, shays, carts and wagons. The pavements teemed. Bella thought how angry everybody looked.

'Aye,' the cabbie agreed. 'Bur tha's no call to go on abahr tit. From London, are ya? There y'are then.'

'Was I going on about it?'

'Y'ad that look, like.'

'You're proud of your town.'

'Am I that!' the cabbie said, with enough sarcasm to wilt lettuce.

The hotel he took her to *was* proud, if a little behind the times, say by fifty years or more. The main rooms were decorated by equestrian portraits of this, that or the other landowner in front of his house, interspersed among canvases depicting wild nature, noble ruins and allegorical nakedness. The clientele comprised businessmen, widows, governesses and militia officers. That day there had been—incredibly—an archery tournament on somewhere called Woodhouse Moor, which turned out to be hardly more than a mile away. Several of the competitors and the outright winner were dining that night but the undisputed centre of attention was a merry man not yet in his forties, with a nose that shone like a nightwatchman's lantern, Tom Emmett of Yorkshire County Cricket Club.

'Would the gentleman sign an autograph for my godson?' a timid woman asked, flourishing the menu.

'Tha can tell t'lad I am no gentleman, missus,' Emmett chortled, scribbling. 'But if he wants to come down to Sheffield for a county match, I shall be happy to shake his hand. And mebbe show him the old sostenutor at work.'

'He will be thrilled,' the godmother promised, with the tiniest flicker of alarm in her voice. Only when she returned to her table did her husband explain (and at some length) that the sostenutor was Emmett's ball that broke back from a length outside off stump, etc., etc. He took the autographed menu card and put it away in his wallet. Bella found the whole incident unintelligible.

'Is it true that there is a factory here that has sheep grazing on its roof?' she asked her dining companion, a frail gentleman on his way to the spa waters of Harrogate. He gave her what Quigley would have described as an old-fashioned look.

'It was once true, yes. Just as in my father's day you could lift pike from the River Aire. I myself have shot for hares on the hill behind the cavalry barracks when a boy. But those times have gone.'

'In the name of progress?'

'So we are told. Is that why you came here, to see the sheep on the roof of Marshall's Mill?'

'I came to walk and sketch in the Dales.'

'There are sheep enough there,' the old man smiled. 'And a more ancient way of life. Do you have a particular destination in mind?'

'I was planning to visit Cruddas, I think it is called. Above Skipton.'

'Is there anything there worth your trouble?' the old man asked. But with just enough in the remark to alert Bella.

'You have heard of it?'

'My name is Foxton,' he murmured.

'Lord Foxton! Please forgive me. We have never met but I had a very particular friend in Yorkshire who spoke of you often and always in the kindest of terms. Yours is the great house a little before Wakefield—I saw it from the train this afternoon.'

'Was your friend Lord Broxtowe? Then you must be what he called his incomparable London rose. Well, well, Mrs Wallis, I see he did not exaggerate. Broxtowe and I were schoolboys together at Eton. To repay your generous compliment, I know that he liked and admired *you* a great deal. The happiest man I ever met. Happy is not quite the right word, either. Blithe would be better.'

Foxton smiled. He pushed back his plate and began to refold his napkin in an absent-minded gesture.

'I should add that he considered you a woman with more moral worth than the Archbishops of York and Canterbury combined. Rather a heavy burden of praise, I should have thought. You will not think me forward, I hope, if I propose a glass of champagne in the little snug they have here?'

'Champagne, my lord?'

'Bubbles,' Lord Foxton explained. 'I would not give the brandy they serve to a dying soldier. Bubbles will suit the occasion better. Come, and you shall tell me about your interest in Cruddas.'

It transpired that Foxton had lead mines in that part of Yorkshire and knew the area well, though the seams were exhausted and he had not visited his property for a dozen years or more.

'It is a very wild and unmanaged landscape you propose to visit. You would do better further east and north, say in Wharfedale, where things are more picturesque by far. Indeed, where Broxtowe had his place. But perhaps you are not going for the picturesque?'

He said this with such delicate insinuation that Bella was forced to face him down.

'There is a woman living there called Lady Ursula Gollinge.'

Foxton inclined his head.

'My tenant—or she would be if little matters like rent had any meaning for her. When the mine was still profitable, I installed the manager—a Swede, incidentally—in what I suppose we might call at a stretch a manor house. The Swede left and the Gollinge woman begged me to let her take it up in his place.'

'But how did she come to hear of it?'

'If you ever find out you must let me know,' Lord Foxton replied drily. 'Is Lady Gollinge a friend of yours?'

'We have never met. It is not very likely we could ever be friends.'

'I am pleased to hear it. The lady is said to be a terrible scandal to her sex, though in fairness I have to say what she gets up to in such a remote place is her own business. Do you read novels at all, Mrs Wallis?'

Bella watched him very carefully but the question appeared to be innocent. Foxton smiled again.

'From all I have heard, what goes on above

63

Cruddas surpasses even the cheapest novel for sensation. Have a care, therefore. You will find Skipton an honest enough place and I can recommend the George Hotel. The vicar is a fund of useless information about birds and snakes and suchlike but a kindly man after his own fashion. The weather is of course execrable.'

'Even in summer, my lord?'

'At any time of the year.'

FIVE

Bella arrived in Skipton on market day with the town *en fête*, the cobbled streets strewn with dung and droppings, the pavements jostling with the families of local farmers, all of them got up in their best. The main street afforded a fine view of the castle which (this being Yorkshire) Bella was three times advised as being the finest example of this particular architecture to be found anywhere in the country.

'Do they have such a thing in Leeds or Bradford? They do not. Now, you say you have come from Leeds this day. And how did you find it? I'll tell thee—a dirtier hole does not exist. Up here, the air is pure. As my old dad says, we should bottle our air and send it down to those unhappy Loiners. You'll have noticed how fresh the streets are.'

This was true; but had much to do with a half gale blowing directly from Lancashire, carrying with it stinging sleet. This gave the faces round about their scrubbed and ruddy looks, as well as causing uproarious accidents, as when a youth's hat flew from his head like a rocketing pheasant and was walked over by a hundred or more sheep.

'And if that don't pay him out for coming it the gentleman, him as has not two ha'ppenies to scratch his arse with and only his poor old mother in work!' a woman shouted with great contentment. 'Yes, his mother washing floors and emptying grates while he laiks about every hour God sends with a bloody flower in his buttonhole and 'lasticated boots!'

'Is he not your Martha's young man?' her companion objected, mildly enough.

'Our Martha's a daft cat, but she aren't that stupid.'

The same two women came into the lounge of the George later, where Martha's mother unwrapped a bit of fish she had bought earlier and passed it to her friend for comment. To Bella's bemusement, they ordered a pint of porter each and fell to talking about haddock. At the next table, two gentlemen in shooting clothes were drinking schooners of sherry and discussing fatstock prices as they had been published in that day's *Yorkshire Post*.

Behind them was a wild-looking woman with blonde-grey corkscrew curls, talking animatedly to a sly-looking girl in a shabby green mantle. Quigley had always insisted to Bella that the eyes were the mirror to the soul. The wild woman had bulging and unblinking eyes that might have indicated unruffled stupidity but for the restless shadows that seemed to flit across their surfaces. A screeching monologue spewed from her box-shaped mouth, something to do with a slight or insult offered earlier in the day. Bella noted how studiously this ugly rant was being ignored, the way some of the same people were forced to ignore the parakeet in the Savile Arms, down by the canal, when they chanced to visit. But there was something more to it than this: the good-natured Skiptonians were acting as one in pretending that the couple were not in the room at all. It took some skill to ignore the physical presence of two other human beings in this way.

'Look at them all,' the woman crowed. 'Their blood three parts sugar, their piggy eyes glistening with lard! Afraid of the dark, afraid of dying. And so very anxious not to be different, not to stand out in the crowd. The herd, Amelia! Animals! Heads down, munching their way through their rotten little lives. With a bit of rutting once in a blue moon, yes, there in the dark with only the wardrobe for witness. And what's it all for?'

'The Empire!' her companion suggested unexpectedly.

'Yes, the Empire! Oh, how grateful we can be that all those lovely black men are shovelling coal for us and holding up umbrellas to keep us from the heat of the sun! While their children starve and their wives are beaten black and blue by soldiers for refusing their drunken and lecherous advances!'

Bella alone watched and listened. Though she still did not realise it, she was looking at Ursula Gollinge. Before she left to venture out into the streets once more, the manager of the hotel gave her a note written in bold slashing characters. It was from the Reverend Mr Sanderson, more or less inviting himself to dinner that night. Or, as he put it, to offer any help he could in deciphering the local character.

* * *

That evening, while dressing, it came to Bella: how many barking mad women were there in Skipton not to make the one she had overheard at lunch Ursula Gollinge? It was the image of the loyal black man shovelling coal while at the same time holding up an umbrella that gave the clue. Bella sat down in her drawers and stays to write all that she could remember of how the woman looked and (more guiltily) the bearing of her young companion. A detail: Lady Ursula was entirely devoid of make-up or jewellery but the girl she called Amelia had so lined her eyes as to draw them out and give her the appearance of a cat. Every finger on both hands was decorated by rings—cheap market rings of Mexican silver, to be sure, set with miniature stones—but a bold enough touch.

As to what they were doing in the hotel that day, this was answered by the night manager when she finally went downstairs to meet Mr Sanderson.

'They come once a week to take a bath,' he explained gloomily.

'Then they have enough of the Empire's ill-gotten gains to book a room.'

'If only,' the manager said. 'Today they were discovered by a Mr Murray in the first-floor front, a gentleman who interests himself in parish churches. He, having been soaked to the skin in his explorations, was about to ease his rheumatism in the bath, when he found it occupied by the lady

67

and her companion. *Together*,' he added in a low voice.

'They were in the bath together?'

'Mr Murray is sixty-four,' the manager said, with a weary shake of his head. 'He says he has never experienced depravity like it, not even he, a man born under a cannon at Waterloo. You will find Mr Sanderson in the residents' lounge, madam. And may I recommend the lamb shank tonight?'

*   *   *

'A curate with his own pony and trap!' Bella mocked gently. Mr Sanderson, lately of Trinity College, Cambridge, took it in good heart.

'The alternative would be a horse, you understand, but the animal that could carry me has yet to be born. It cheers people to see their curate carried about like a circus freak. I am brother to the Hottentot Venus, Mrs Wallis.'

Mr Sanderson was certainly a very large young man. Of only medium height, his fat was lumped onto him, so that for example his hands (which were girlishly delicate) peeped from under rolls of fat that threatened to overwhelm them. His thighs were each greater in girth than Bella's waist and when he laughed, his whole body shook like a blancmange. But Mr Sanderson had beautifully alert eyes. Lord Foxton had sent him a telegraph advising him of Bella's presence in the George and now here he was at dinner, as shrewd a mind as existed in the hotel that night. His manners were impeccable.

'Will you not tell me how you came into your curacy?' Bella asked.

'Oh, but don't you think the church needs jolly and uncomplicated men, Mrs Wallis? The parishioners call me Friar Tuck, which is very pleasing. What's needed in this vocation is a sort of holy innocence. People admire the vicar—Mr Mountain—for his learned ways and rather austere manners. They like me for a poor fat lad, as they style me, one who can never say boo to a goose. As a consequence I am told things enough to make a sailor blush.'

'Do you know why I am here, Mr Sanderson?'

'I am anxious to discover the reason,' the curate responded politely.

'Do you happen to know Lady Ursula Gollinge?'

'I see,' Sanderson said.

'You do know her?'

The curate left off eating long enough to spread his hands in the international gesture which the moderately sane use to indicate dismay in the face of what verges on the incomprehensible.

'Here, in the more remote parts of the tops, as they call them, people are known as much by their sins as their virtues. For example, Raybould, a name as famous as any in the Craven District. A farmer. When his wife died in 1855, he took leave of absence from the human race. Nobody has actually seen Walter Raybould since he was fifty-odd years old, not so much as a stolen glimpse.'

'But then what is his sin, to make him so notorious?'

'He killed his wife with a hatchet. Before two witnesses,' Sanderson explained calmly. 'The police have looked for him a hundred times since—in newspaper jargon, they have combed the moors. He has never been apprehended. Some say he lives underground. Children believe he can transform himself at will, say into a stoat, or a hawk.'

'We are in Transylvania!' Bella exclaimed wonderingly.

'Wouldn't it seem so?' the curate smiled.

'But what has this man to do with Lady Gollinge?'

Sanderson laid down his knife and fork with some regret and pushed away his empty plate.

'In practical terms, nothing. I use him as an illustration of the power the local folk have to reshape the world according to their lights. Raybould has decreed his own punishment. When he dies, there will be no burial and no fine words spoken over him. The people understand that. He has gone to live outside the tribe.'

'And so, it might be said, has Lady Gollinge,' Bella suggested.

'Maybe. But Raybould has touched something very ancient in the penance he has set himself. Put beside his example, Ursula Gollinge is merely a wilful and vexatious interloper. His is a human tragedy. She is a raree show.'

'Hasn't she too a right to live as she wishes?'

'Indeed,' Sanderson replied. 'But whether it earns her a scrap of respect is another matter. Decency is a virtue held very high among country people. She has none. I may pity her but those of the common people who have crossed her path despise her.'

'One last question, then: *do* you pity her?'

'Why,' the kindly and jolly Mr Sanderson said, forgetting his calling for a moment and speaking like the undergraduate he so recently was, 'I

70

have never held another human being in such contempt.'

And so they sat; and so they ate pudding. Bella ended the evening better off by the loan of the curate's pony and trap—and the promise of a boy, Alfie Stannard, to drive it for her. She was grateful, too, for a hand-drawn map and some useful advice about the very few inns to be had in the district around Cruddas; but what stuck in her mind was this last remark of Mr Sanderson's and the unequivocal vehemence with which it was delivered.

'Unless you have personal dealings with Lady Gollinge, I would keep well away. There may be entertainment in the spectacle she makes of herself, the way that village simpletons are sometimes cruelly advertised. But truly, Mrs Wallis, the lady is beneath your consideration. There is nothing worth your interest here.'

'Aren't all stories worth the telling?'

'I believe not.'

They said goodnight on the steps of the George, with the arrangement that the curate would drive himself back to his lodgings and in the morning the boy Alfie would return with the trap. The wind had dropped a little and the rain abated. Rags of white clouds moved across the roofs of Skipton, lit by an almost full moon. Though it was hardly past eleven, not a soul stirred. When Bella went to bed, the last sound she heard before sleep was that of a fox's dry coughing in the castle grounds.

She dreamed of Philip. Skipton had become a town on the Danube and its citizens Turks. Bella was looking for him in a crowded souk filled with sinister-looking characters, a place all the more

71

frightful for birds, great swirls of them, swooping and diving. They were, she judged shakily, ravens. Guards on the castle roof were firing at them with impossibly long and old-fashioned muskets. Lord Foxton was in the dream, as was Mr Sanderson, who seemed to find the whole thing a cause for merriment. Easy for these two: they sat on cushions in a scented courtyard, drinking sherbet, while the world came to pieces outside.

It occurred to Bella that the place to look for Philip was down by the river and she ran there through rustling stalks of what she took to be maize, jumping sticks that terror taught her might also be snakes. She was not naked, but her feet were bare. When she looked down, she saw that she was wearing only a nightgown—the very nightgown in which she slept that night. The distant gunfire she heard could not possibly come from the shooting of ravens: the city was in a state of insurrection. She began to smell smoke.

When at last she found Philip, he was standing on the stern deck of a departing steamer, dressed in a cream suit. It seemed impossible that he did not see or hear her howling at him to turn back; but after a moment or two he sauntered away down the thrumming deck.

'He has gone,' an obliging old man in a turban explained.

*   *   *

Though the same moon that shone over the moors of the West Riding illuminated Westphalia, there was nothing romantic about Philip's landscape. Midnight in Essen disclosed a bleak network of

72

railway lines, drifting in and out of definition as banks of yellow smoke moved about uneasily, generated from God knew where and seemingly with a mind of their own. A cruelly ugly iron bridge over the tracks was lit by a dozen darting naphtha lamps. Earlier in the night a man had hanged himself from its central span, some said a poor workman laid off by one of the foundries, some a farmer looking for his daughter—and finding her.

One of the figures on the bridge detached itself and sauntered towards Philip, who was half concealed in the shadows of a grimy warehouse.

'It is Wachter,' he murmured.

'You don't know that.'

'I know what the police told me. So now they ask what does an elderly clerk in the plans office of the mighty Krupps Works think he is about, trying on a hemp necktie? It being our friend Wachter of course, he was wearing his best suit and newest boots. There was a briefly held theory that he had been attending a funeral, the poor fellow. But anyway, suicide.'

'Did he leave a note?' Philip asked. His companion's rich laugh was so loud and so out of place that several heads turned on the bridge.

'You are not quite as stupid as you look, Herr Westland.'

'We should search his lodgings. We should go now.'

'That is being done. But what if his note was in the nature of a detailed confession? And what if it is not propped against a greasy coffee pot in his lodgings but waiting in Herr Krupp's in-tray? Have you thought of that?'

'Let us meet again at breakfast.'

'Here? In Essen?' the man cried incredulously. 'By dawn I intend to be very far away indeed. You are not trying to rob a shopkeeper: this is Krupp you are dealing with. Steel is a ruthless business. Herr Krupp has a policy towards industrial spies. They are crushed like mice under one of his steam hammers. You have failed, Englishman. And now your life is forfeit.'

'You have a gift for melodrama, Herr Furst,' Philip said amiably enough. 'If you are planning to leave Essen tonight, I need hardly tell you that your silence will be taken for granted by my principals in London. You have already been paid well—not for your loyalty, of course, but discretion. Should that ever desert you, things would turn out very badly for both you and your family.'

Herr Furst studied the shadowed face in front of him, uncertain how to respond. This shambling Englishman, for all his easy command of German, was quite clearly an amateur at the game. Yet there was something about him Furst could not completely dismiss. The reason had to do with the one they called Alcock. Alcock, it was said, never left London but was known all over Europe for a feral ruthlessness. Furst had often tried to picture what he looked like and always came up with the uncomfortable image of one of those stolid unimaginative Englishmen to be found staring down the foreigners in Baden-Baden, like men inspecting cattle. A thought struck him: Maybe Westland *was* Alcock. Maybe he was being played for a fool.

'I have no wish to cause the slightest anxiety to your principals,' he muttered.

'They will be pleased to hear that,' Philip replied gravely.

'We could perhaps even travel back to London together?'

Or, Furst thought, I could put my mind at ease by breaking your neck here and now. He was in a panic. What he had said about the Krupp family's power to silence their opponents was a commonplace; if anything the son was more vindictive than the father. Nor was it simply a local matter. The dossier in question—the one poor Wachter had been suborned to steal or copy—was a commission given to Krupp by the Kriegsmarine. Which was to say, in the end, Bismarck.

Looking past Furst's shoulder Philip saw two policemen marching towards them across the bridge. Raising his voice, he thanked Furst profusely for such a handsome reunion dinner and begged to be remembered to Marthe and the little ones! Next year in Dusseldorf, that was for sure! Vogel would be there, and old Pappi Mundt. *Then* they would toast the regiment three times three!

Philip walked away, his hands shaking, but with enough sangfroid left to pause for a moment to light a cigar. There was a cab twenty yards ahead of him and the driver cracked his whip over the sleeping horse's head when he saw the match flare. A drunken whore scooted from the interior of the cab and stumbled into an unlit alley. Philip took her place. The leather bench she had vacated was warm.

'Where to?' the cabbie croaked. But before he could answer, Furst's face appeared at the open window, followed immediately by a blinding flash. Philip felt a bolt of pain in his shoulder and fell sideways onto the horsehair cushions. The bullet had passed clean through him, raising clouds of dust from the ancient upholstery. The cab rocked as the driver lashed his horse uphill over the cobbles, standing up on his box and shouting blue murder. Inside, Philip smelled gun smoke, burning cloth from the cigar that had lodged in the folds of his suit—and blood.

SIX

Alfie Stannard turned out to be a pleasant boy with excellent manners. Bella judged him to be seventeen or so, lean and sinewy with bright red hair and skin freckled like a thrush's egg. He wore chequered trousers and a patched linen jacket but it was his footwear that drew the eye. Bella was fairly convinced that his once-elegant boots, their soles as thin as paper, were cast-offs from his patron, Mr Sanderson. Fashioned for nothing more demanding than a walk across Trinity Great Court, perhaps to go as far as the post office or the Blue Boar, here in Skipton they were as out of place as a Chinaman's slippers. Alfie wore them with pride.

That he had also fallen in love with Bella at first sight was obvious to them both, yet he managed to get his feelings under control enough to drive her up the valley to Cruddas Bridge. There they rested the horse and sat down by the river on table-sized boulders, watching the water. Bella was intrigued. Alfie had suddenly grown jumpy, afflicted by nervous yawning and what Mrs Venn would have called a bad case of the fidgets. He pointed out the dark shadows of trout but his heart wasn't in it.

'Didn't think this was the place you wanted to come.'

'Yet it all seems very peaceful,' Bella said in an attempt to calm him. And so it was if you liked silence and emptiness. They had passed the last drystone walls more than a mile back. The bridge was solid enough but it was the only indication that man had otherwise laid one stone upon another in these parts. Cruddas was nowhere to be seen. When asked where it was, Alfie pointed carelessly to the north.

'Can you not smell it?'

'I cannot. Is that how you find your way round up here—by sniffing places out? Is the nose your compass?'

As soon as she said this, Bella realised how fatuous she sounded. Philip would never have said anything so patronising, nor would he have noticed much if the boy's feet were stuffed into squelching marrows, or sandals made from string and cowpats. Alfie's mildly reproving glance was like a punch to the ribs.

'You can't smell a bone fire? Someone's burning summat.'

'Garden refuse, for example?'

'You mean like grass clippings and that? Nah.'

'Something more serious, then.'

'Just a fire, like. Thought you might smell it.'

He pulled a wet stalk of grass and chewed like a goat.

'Aren't many that come this high up,' he explained, 'except for the gentlemen from Leeds and maybe Halifax who fish. Right now it's too bright and the sky is too high.'

'You know about trout, Alfie?'

'Every boy does.'

'And do you come here to fish yourself?'

Amazingly, he blushed. Dropped his head and fell to examining his hands. Watched Bella from under his lashes.

'They'd be *your* friends,' he mumbled.

'Who? Who are you talking about?'

'The ladies that live over the ridge yonder.'

'What ladies can you mean?'

He pointed and resumed his blushing.

'Do you mean these waters are theirs? They've turned you off, have they?'

'No, no, oh, no. They're nobody to tell local people what they can and can't do. No, I was thinking on something else.'

'Can you tell me what that is?'

'Best not to mention,' he mumbled.

'You have the makings of a novelist, Alfie. You can see now that nothing will do but you tell me what this other thing is. I am on fire with curiosity.'

'I spoke out of turn,' he said.

'Don't be so gormless,' Bella snapped. 'I have not come all this way to admire the landscape. Those two ladies interest me quite as much as they do you.'

He flapped the remark away with bony hands and then burst into snotting tears, enough to startle even the horse. Bella was amazed—here was a solid enough country boy with his head in his hands and sobbing like a girl.

'You won't tell Vicar or Mr Sanderson?' he wept.

'Of course not. But you haven't said what it is I

must keep secret.'

He wiped his tears away with the back of his wrist and stood.

'You had best see for yourself,' he muttered thickly and began walking downstream. Bella followed. There came a point in the river where they might cross, jumping from boulder to boulder, and this they did, at the expense of Bella's shoes and stockings. Once across, the boy pointed to a steep bank. A curlew cried piteously over their heads.

Only fifty yards from the road another country began, greeny-grey and largely featureless. What should have been a fine prospect of the Aire Valley running east to Leeds was obscured by a huge limestone bluff, maybe a mile off. The Pennines rose to the west in a green wall. There was plenty of sky to admire but not much else. The grass was as short as a lawn but scratchy and (as she discovered soon enough) filthy dirty. Dark banks of bilberries grew along the less exposed slopes and there were two or three forlorn stands of what looked like blackthorn trees.

They scrambled for half an hour before Alfie drew her down beside a little outcrop of rock. She was surprised how grateful she was for the respite. Sweat ran out of her hair and her eyes hurt from so much uninterrupted brightness. She found that for some minutes past she had been holding his hand and this she now disengaged, feeling alarmingly foolish and girlish about it, too. The tweed suit that had looked so well in the pony and trap clung to her hips and thighs as damp as any bath-towel. Alfie smiled at her.

' 'Tis easier for a man, perhaps.'

'Why is the grass so dirty?' she asked.

'Mills,' he answered. 'Over in Lancashire, like. Come winter, the snow is grey.'

'And why have we come here? To this particular spot?'

'You'll see,' he promised.

She lay back on the grass and closed her eyes, very conscious of him as an animal presence, child though he was. What had seemed like an oppressive silence was gradually resolving into a story—the curlew was still there but she could also hear the wind in the grass and even the very faint and syncopated sound of water tumbling through rocks. A very long way off, but carried to her by a trick of the wind, came the thrum of the looms at Slingsby's Mill, maddening to those who worked there but here no more than a whisper.

And then suddenly, unmistakably, a woman's voice cawing like a rook. Alfie laid his hand warningly on her forearm.

'Don't sit up,' he whispered. 'Don't show yourself. If you was to roll over onto your front—but slowly, like—'

At first she could see nothing. His hand was in the small of her back, pressing her down to the ground. They lay like lovers. Alfie took her finger and gently pointed it towards the low ground in the distance.

'Keep still,' he said. 'They are in that little beck. You see yon rock that looks like a cow?'

She did not, but then Ursula Gollinge obliged her by climbing up onto it, maybe a hundred yards away. After a moment, a younger woman joined her. There was something odd about the pair of them that Bella was slow to grasp. And then it dawned on her. Both women were stark naked and the sticks they seemed to be carrying were bows and arrows. They paused for a moment and appeared to look straight at Bella. Then plunged back down out of sight. The next time they appeared they were a hundred yards further off, showing their rumps like rabbits.

*   *   *

It did nothing for Alfie's peace of mind that Bella commanded him to take the trap further along the road to look for the women's house. She too was anxious she might be tipping her hand by doing so. On the other hand, what she had seen out on the fells begged for some sort of context. They crossed the bridge and struggled up a boulder-strewn ridge to Cruddas.

The entire village was crammed into a high-sided valley and comprised a single street of miners' cottages with stone roofs and tiny windows, more like pigpens than human dwellings. The few Cruddas folk who were about in the streets offered the traditional Yorkshire welcome given to incomers, which is to say they turned their backs on the pony and trap, some of them going so far as to face the wall until it passed. Bella took her cue from Alfie and stared straight ahead. Trickles of sweat ran down her ribs.

'There is the house,' the boy whispered, pointing with his chin down a steep dirt track. Even if they had wanted to visit they could not, for a hundred yards along the track a huge tree had been felled to block the way and left to rot, branches and all. Beyond, Bella saw the roof and yard of a fairly substantial building. Lashed to the chimney stack was a drunken pole, bearing—in place of a flag—a string of bones and feathers. Round about the yard there lay bits and pieces of what she assumed had once been mining machinery now glowing red with rust. The source of the smoke was explained. Lady Gollinge was not disposing of her grass clippings but burning a filthy mattress and—even more scandalously—a horsehair sofa. Bella shuddered.

'I have seen enough,' she mumbled faintly. 'This is a gate to hell.'

*   *   *

An hour later, they sat in the garden of a single-storey inn further down the valley, eating wonderfully nutty bread and thick slices of ham. Chickens scratched about under the table and several cats stalked. After Cruddas, the pure ordinariness of the scene acted on Bella like strong drink. This too was a poor and forsaken place but it was recognisably human. There were even little touches of ambition—a painted milk churn, pansies in a pot.

'How close have you been to them?' she asked, after a long silence. Alfie knew to whom she was referring.

'They have come closer to where we was earlier,' he admitted. 'Much closer once or twice. Say from here to that yew.'

'Did they discover you?'

He looked at her with something of pity in his eyes.

'I aren't that stupid, am I?'

'And you think they saw us today, however?'

'Saw *you*,' Alfie chuckled. 'She wor looking straight at you, the old bag. She won't like what she saw.'

'And what's she going to do about it?' Bella scoffed.

'Them Cruddas folk are tough, right tough. But they're all scared of her.'

'Look at me, Alfie. Do I look scared to you?'

'Not yet you don't.'

'And the nakedness and such. Do you have some idea of what that is all about?'

'They were hunting. With bows and arrows. The young girl, she's Amelia from off the barges. Did you see the warpaint?'

'Is that what it was? And if you fall to blushing again I shall stick you with this knife.'

'That old thing? Couldn't cut water.' But he found some courage and touched his nipple briefly. 'Here? Round here? That is all painted black, huge black. Old Gollinge, she has a white face, like a skellington. 'Melia likewise. Feathers and that. But not a stitch of cloth anywhere. I dream about them,' he added unnecessarily.

'But what are they hunting?'

'Rabbits. I've seen them try to shoot at pheasants on the wing, the barmpots. Always stark bollock . . . always naked. Same as all the singing they do, the wailing. And dancing.'

'That must be worth seeing,' Bella said absently. When she saw that she made Alfie flinch, she patted his hand. 'You are a good boy to have taken me. Would you like the rest of my ham?'

He took it and stuffed it in his pocket.

'You would never do a thing like that?' he asked with a sudden arch smile, indicating they were in

83

some sense co-conspirators. 'I mean, run about covered in paint?'

'You have my word on it,' Bella responded gravely, convulsing Alfie with silent laughter. 'But tomorrow we must get closer. I need to know what tribe they belong to. Would that suit you, too?'

'I think she knows who you are,' he whispered.

'And how could that be?'

'She has powers, no doubt about it.'

The hotel, Bella thought. Someone at the hotel has tipped her the wink, perhaps the lugubrious and put-upon manager.

'*I* have powers,' she declared grandly, patting Alfie on the head and then caressing his cheek. Earlier, she had asked the stunned landlady for coffee and now this buxom woman came out with what she imagined might be the next best thing, two earthenware mugs of nettle tea. The curlew that seemed to follow them round hung in the sky and for a moment life seemed to be good. Even the sweet treacly stink that floated from the inn's interior seemed apt and charming. Bella spoilt it for both the boy and the no-nonsense innkeeper by smoking, a scandalous way for a lady to be going on and something the two of them equated with distant manners in a part of England never to be imagined. In other words, London.

*   *   *

Well, Henry Ellis Margam asked, what did you expect? You are indeed far from London and—at least so far as discovering a suitable plot for a novel bearing my name—quite out of kilter with the modern taste. Madness has its own aesthetic. A

84

beautiful woman maddened by grief, or a child struck dumb by a single fateful turn of fortune's wheel—both these are quite permissible when properly brought forward. But two women running about stark naked in the depths of Yorkshire is another matter. And the bows and arrows are a poor touch, one might even say a cheap effect. The castle at the bottom of this street is a far better location for a sensational tale. Let us imagine: Lady Mauleverer discovers a hidden passage in the picture gallery that leads . . . that leads somewhere or other . . . and is forced to keep this ghastly discovery secret from her husband, who, lamed in a recent riding accident . . .

Bella threw down her pen in disgust. Downstairs in the hotel a wedding party was celebrating uproariously and she had elected to take her evening meal in her room. She had accordingly drunk two-thirds of a bottle of Niersteiner and smoked as much as any militia captain bored by his comrades but too lazy to make a sortie from quarters.

Both windows were wide open and the long dusk was finally giving way to night. What Lady Mauleverer needed to do was to brick up the secret passages in her castle to prevent her adorable husband from disappearing down them on his mysterious errands, buy herself a completely new outfit, give up the office in Fleur de Lys Court and go to live by the sea. Buy a telescope, take up painting, collect fossils, anything that had nothing to do with pen and paper. Take the inkwell and hurl it into the waves. Slam the door in Henry Ellis Margam's face and forget he ever existed.

She was startled by the dry crack of a pebble

85

flung against her window. When she peered out she saw a moonstruck Alfie standing in the roadway in front of the hotel.

'What is it?' she called.

'At what time tomorrow?' he called back shyly.

'Alfie, it is near enough midnight.'

'I know. But they won't let me up to your room.'

'Go home and go to bed.'

'If you say so. But listen—I've had a right good idea.'

'Excellent!' Bella said. 'Tell me tomorrow. Be here at ten.'

There are things to do in a hotel bedroom that seem strange and difficult which in a home would pass completely unremarked. Cleaning one's teeth, hair-brushing, even reading in bed—all these became minor battles with mirrors and lamps, rucked carpets and inadequate curtains. When Bella finally flopped into bed, she felt exhausted but horribly wide awake. At home in Orange Street she would have padded round the house in her bare feet, even going as far as the kitchens to make tea. The mere act of thinking this made her homesick.

There came a point in every Bella adventure, before it became a Margam book, when it was sensible to ask no more questions of the raw material. She was not a detective, after all, any more than was Wilkie Collins or any of the other novelists in her field. She had set herself the task to find out more about Ursula Gollinge; discovering her as some sort of Red Indian out on the moors was revelation enough. Were she to go on and uncover some other madness, like plans for an attack on Leeds Town Hall by means of a hot air balloon, how much more would she actually learn? The one question she wanted to put to Lady Gollinge was foolishly querulous: What have you to do with my beloved Philip Westland?

The answer seemed obvious. It was against all probability the two had ever met. Bella sat up in bed and tried to punch the pillow soft, putting more bad temper into the effort than was ladylike.

There was a surreptitious scratching at the door. She got out of bed and for want of another weapon found her boot. Opened the door a crack, ready for battle.

Out in the corridor was an amiable-looking young man in his shirtsleeves, wearing a woman's hat and with his boots knotted round his neck. His socks had holes.

'I do beg your pardon,' he said with the elaborate courtesy of the roaring drunk. 'I was looking for Myrtle Longstaff. You are not her.'

As Bella closed the door on him, the woman's hat explained itself. The young man was a piece of flotsam from the wedding reception.

*   *   *

There was blood on the woman's apron and Philip supposed she had been slaughtering chickens. This was a farmhouse, he judged, or perhaps the summer kitchen to a larger building. The air was as thick as gravy and the flies that crawled across his face and neck seemed drunk on it. He could hear someone sawing wood nearby; further off, what might be the herding of cows. Daylight hurt his eyes. It slowly dawned on him that the blood on the woman's clothes was his own.

'Where am I?' he asked.

'My man will talk to you when he comes in.'

'Where is he now?'

'What does it matter where he is?' the woman shrilled. 'But if you don't lie still, you will start to bleed like a pig again. Be grateful you are not out in the ditch, where we found you.'

'Where is this place?'

'Naturally, this is heaven and we are angels.'

She held up his head and poured something disgusting down his throat, something he racked his brains to recognise. Finally it came to him. Milk.

'I have been shot,' he explained unnecessarily. 'I don't know how I came here but I have money—'

He stopped. They knew that. The woman's smile was sardonic. She wiped his lips by rubbing her thumb across them.

'Everybody has a story they want to tell others,' she said. 'We will listen to yours later. Meanwhile, sleep.'

'Sleep!'

'Why not?' she said. 'It's not so difficult.'

SEVEN

Alfie's bubblingly bright idea was to take Bella to see Duxbury. At first she supposed this to be a nearby village; but Duxbury, who had shed his first name like a snake, was that inherently contradictory thing, a popular hermit. Not a local man, mind, for who could take seriously anyone daft enough to live in a limestone cave unless he came from exotic foreign parts—in his case, Woodhouse Street in Leeds. Five years ago, Duxbury had walked out on his hole-in-the-wall tobacconist kiosk opposite the Chemical Works and, after a year's adventures along the way, found his new station in life. In his wake, he left behind a wife, two daughters and five grandchildren. Bella was profoundly depressed by this story.

'It's a wonder he's still alive,' she commented sourly.

'Oh, it's a right roomy cave,' Alfie assured her. 'And Mr Sanderson says that folk used to live there in the Ice Age when the woolly mammals roamed.'

'I was trying to indicate how it's a great wonder his wife hasn't come up here and stabbed him to death with her umbrella.'

'It's no small thing being a hermit,' Alfie answered indignantly. 'He muses on things, is what he does. The older people go to see him when they've got a problem. My *mother* has been to see him.'

'And what was her problem?

'To do with her insides,' Alfie muttered.

And this is it, Bella thought: I am trapped in a very bad dream, such as comes at a noisy picnic after too much sun and a glass too many of wine. This child is the will-o'-the-wisp that is drawing me on. Madwomen running naked over the fells, and now a hermit. When he caught her scowling at him, Alfie managed to look pained and innocent, like a child being scolded for making up stories about bogeymen under the bed.

It was a mild morning with wan sunshine. Bella was entertaining the boy to a cup of coffee in the orchard garden of the hotel, where a convention of wasps was also meeting. It was her fixed London habit to swipe at things that buzzed and it did nothing for her temper that Alfie seemed not to notice the wasps, to the extent of letting one crawl across the orange hairs on the back of his wrist.

'You don't want to get them angry,' he advised.

'I want them to know that I am angry.'

In an effort to placate her, he picked up the wasp that was examining his shirt cuff and nipped its head off between his thumb and forefinger. Bella winced. The day had already got off to a bad start when he told her with artless candour that the coffee in front of him was the first he had ever tasted. Didn't like it much, neither. It stuck to your teeth, like. The hermit business came after.

'What do you think we can learn from this man?' she asked.

'Duxbury knows all,' Alfie promised. 'And he has a right good view of that valley where the naked ladies do their hunting.'

'You've spoken to him about that?'

'I might have mentioned it,' Alfie confessed, blushing.

They were interrupted by the arrival of Mr Sanderson, wafting into the orchard like a great black balloon, carrying his Bible under one arm and encumbered by a string bag of sheet music and a pound or so of onions.

'I came to see how you are getting on,' he boomed in that jolly way that parsons have. 'Alfie, be a dear and fetch me some coffee. And perhaps a doughnut or two.'

Alfie was only too anxious to scoot off, though not before throwing Bella an imploring glance, easy enough to interpret: the less said about

Ursula Gollinge, the better. But Mr Sanderson seemed to have other things on his mind. He was having his usual problem with chairs. He examined the one in front of him with suspicion, jiggled the back, and sat. There was a satisfying shriek as his mighty bottom tested the joints and then he leaned back with content. The legs sank into the turf like tent pegs.

'You are looking well, Mrs Wallis,' he smiled. 'I hope that boy is proving useful. He told me this morning he wished you to meet Duxbury.'

Sanderson by day was a slightly more formidable presence. She could account for this by supposing that he was in working mode (hence the Bible and possibly the onions, a gift to some housebound or indigent parishioner); or she could react to a faint steeliness in his voice that was not there before.

'We were discussing just that proposal when you arrived.'

'Yes,' Sanderson said. 'It is a pleasant enough drive and the weather is wonderfully clement. If you have the time, nothing could be more agreeable, I am sure.'

'I am not here on holiday, however. Alfie believes Mr Duxbury to be a valuable fund of local knowledge.'

'I doubt it,' Sanderson said shortly. 'What is agreeable about the expedition is the scenery. Particularly lovely chestnuts along the road.'

'You mean to warn me, however.'

'My dear Mrs Wallis, it is no part of my duty to warn you of anything. You are here for a purpose greater than sightseeing, I can see that, though I do not enquire what it is. I will simply say that sometimes it is better to let sleeping dogs lie.'

'Is that how parish duties are conceived here in Yorkshire?'

He flushed. Like a good curate, he was too astute to lose his temper completely. Instead, he steepled his fingers and touched them to his lips, all the while looking at her with a very level gaze indeed.

'Pay me the compliment of believing I have your best interests at heart,' he said finally. 'You saw Lady Gollinge and her companion yesterday, I understand.'

'In astonishing circumstances.'

'Alfie told me. I am sorry to have you witness that. It is a great scandal.'

'Everything has its explanation, however. Do you have views, Mr Sanderson?'

'Views? They have put themselves out of reach of normal society, this much we know. I don't think it is likely to turn out to be for any very sinister reason. They do not like the world as they find it. Nor do many others, albeit of different stripe. And so: let it be.'

'Their behaviour doesn't interest you?'

'It does not.'

'And Mr Duxbury?'

He flapped his hands, as though shooing away a fly.

'A harmless buffoon. I should add you have by no means exhausted Alfie's store of local eccentrics. According to him, Old Mother Marriot, a whiskery lady who smokes a pipe down by the canal, can spell warts and drive away the devil from a fractious child. Sergeant Lowden, late of the Green Jackets, speaks in tongues. It is said he can stop clocks just by looking at them. And so on.

This is not society London, Mrs Wallis. We are neighbourly with our madmen, if you wish to see it that way.'

'I will put it to you bluntly, Mr Sanderson. What might I discover about Lady Gollinge in particular that is best left undisturbed?'

'To speak bluntly? Towering stupidity and self-regard. Most of all and much more serious, a vast emptiness. A desert.'

'I have never seen a desert,' Bella said.

'But then of course she has. In Australia, I understand.'

It suddenly fell into place: the nakedness, the tribal markings, bows and arrows, hunting and gathering. It was as though Sanderson had known about this all along but despaired of her making the connection for herself. Bella stared at him incredulously. The curate permitted himself something of an un-Christian smirk.

'I have never seen these women out on the moor but any number of small boys have had their bottoms reddened for spying. The children think of them as grown-ups playing at Red Indians. Their parents take a more sanguine view.'

'You did not think to tell me about this at the very beginning?'

He dropped his eyes to poke about in his string bag.

'These onions are for old Mrs Jeffreys. She eats them raw to ward off the cold. Mrs Jeffreys was a babe in arms at the Peterloo Massacre. Her mother was sabred by a dragoon, you understand, and her father carried her as far from Manchester as was possible for a man with no work and sought by the police and their informers at every turn. I do not say this in any political sense, but Lady Gollinge is not fit to lick her boots. Ah, here is Alfie with my doughnuts.'

'You don't see a small mystery with these two women that is worth your solving, Mr Sanderson?'

'Whenever I want to be taxed by mysteries, Mrs Wallis, I open the piano lid and take a turn at Schumann.'

Prig! Bella almost shouted in his face.

*   *   *

The walk to Duxbury's cave was along the foot of an impressive limestone reef. Sheep and the locals had made quite a little path and the going was steep but easy. The hermit greeted them with great good humour, pulling Bella up by her wrists into a roomy opening in the rock. Presents were offered and accepted—a few links of sausages, a box of vegetables, a pound of tea and some twist tobacco.

Duxbury was a very unbiblical hermit. Despite his long hair and straggling beard he managed to persist with something of his former character, which was that of a chatty and whimsical tobacconist in good standing with his customers. There were certainly difficulties in his appearance to overcome, as for instance the woman's burgundy velvet frock he wore over some disgraceful trousers; and the bulkiness that came as a consequence of sporting two short jackets, one worn over the other. He smelled—the whole cave smelled—of wood smoke and this had also coloured his face yellow. On his hands were grey woollen mittens.

Duxbury smiled. 'You have come from London,

94

I perceive. The Queen is sad. Today she lost a silver thimble and all the fine ladies are searching for it. No,' he chuckled, as if witnessing the scene, 'it is not *there*.'

'It has rolled under the piano,' Bella said firmly, astonishing Alfie and causing Duxbury to look at her in a different light.

'Take a pew,' he suggested, indicating a shelf of rock. 'The lad will mash us some tea. There is neither milk nor sugar in the house but you won't mind that.'

'You call this your house?'

'I speak as I have always spoke. It is my dwelling, if you prefer that way of looking at it. Yes, you can say that people of our class live in dwellings. You are looking at me out the corner of your eyes, widow-woman.'

Spencer Gore, all-England tennis champion, could not have put her on the back foot more successfully.

'How did you know I was widowed?'

Duxbury made little twittering gestures with his fingers. They were perhaps meant to indicate information that was carried on the ether.

'Is there no man in my life, then?'

'For sure! How could there not be, you as young and beautiful as you are? But there is trouble there, too.'

'What sort of trouble?'

Duxbury smiled and found a new job for his hands, palms up, as he once might have done when a customer commented on a week of rain.

'Isn't the heart nowt but a cabinet with hidden drawers? Who can say what troubles a man must keep therein?'

'Therein?' Bella scoffed.

'Therein,' the hermit repeated nonchalantly.

He was less flowery on the domestic economy of living alone in the cleft of a rock. Duxbury did not hunt rabbits with a bow and arrow like his neighbours: he trapped them with the help of a spool of silk line someone had bought him to catch trout by. Nettles grew a little way off and he enjoyed those for what he called their roughage. Docks would not kill you if boiled down to a green paste; and dandelions (though hard to find) had a fresh nip to them that was delicious. He had even feasted on wild strawberries in his time. And—as this morning—nobody who came to see him ever came empty-handed. He showed Bella his two tin saucepans and an iron kettle, his kitchen knife and coal hammer. There was a cabinet of curios arranged on rocks at the back of the cave—a mouse skull, ram's horns, a snakeskin, some blunt and orange teeth from the carcass of a sheep. Wrapped in a scrap of cloth were a belt buckle and a tin watch with a broken glass.

'These were Raybould the murderer's,' he said.

'He is dead?'

'Oh, I found *him* in a beck. Down there, where the mine is. I buried him two years back. Leastways, covered him in rocks. So now he is a waterfall.'

'And you told no one? Not the police or anyone?'

'The police,' the hermit scolded gently. 'I think you are a free spirit, lass, same as me. What are the police to such as us? I have yet to meet a philosophical one.'

'Do you know how he died?'

'He was quite unable to help me on that.'

Duxbury's smile had the same power of insinuation as smoke or water. There is no smoke without fire, Bella thought wildly. For all his mask of amiability this is a dangerous hermit.

'How did you know I was a widow?' she repeated abruptly. 'And the truth this time.'

'It needed no special gift,' Duxbury replied. 'Alfie thinks I am a bit of a wizard, don't you, old lad? I am not. For thirty years I stood behind a counter selling folk stuff. I were very bad at it, for I cared less about the money than the look in their eye or the shape their mouths took when speaking. Each one was a walking history book. The money was just bits of copper or silver. Only a fool thinks about money. You're a lass that understands all that.'

'What else can you see in my face, then?'

'You're a wilful woman, that much anyone can see. You have no children and it says summat about you that you appear not to have paid much mind to that fact. You're not rich but then again you're not poor neither. You'd as soon live with women as with men.'

'You're very impudent, Mr Duxbury.'

'Aye, well,' the hermit smiled, taking his tea from Alfie and wafting it cool with a mittened hand. Living alone had given him the gift of switching off. He was waiting, Bella knew he was waiting, and try as she might, she could not bring herself to stay silent.

'And the man who is in my life now?'

'Is in some trouble,' Duxbury said calmly, fixing her with his pale blue eyes. 'He is that. Just at the moment, like, I would say he is arse over tip in

97

calamity.'

*   *   *

Fog. No, not fog but clouds, the kind you look down on from mountain peaks. Philip knew he was nowhere near a mountain and that the lowering crag in front of him was a kneeling man. Better in the end to say fog. Mental fog. Better. It was the thing gnawing at his shoulder that was causing the problem. If he had the strength he would brush it away. But then all his strength was taken up in stopping his eyes from rolling.

'Listen to me,' the kneeling man said, slapping Philip's face gently to get his attention. 'My wife thinks we should rob you more and then kill you.'

'You already have everything,' Philip mumbled. His tongue seemed to have turned to wool in his mouth and he was finding it hard to hear himself speak for the singing in his ears. Stinging sweat ran into his eyes.

'Yes, that is true,' the man said. 'I have your watch, your wallet, your excellent boots. When people stay at hotels, they pay for their room, don't they? Ach so, this is not a proper hotel and we are poor. But not stupid. You have been talking in your sleep, Englishman. At first we thought you were from Berlin, such correct German, so fine an accent. But now we know.'

'Then you know my friends are coming for me.'

William Kennett, he thought deliriously. And Bella. Bella naked in the bedroom, turning a hip towards the door, a hairbrush in her hand. She is coming for me. She cannot abide fog. Or woolliness. He smacked his lips together a few

98

times to bring his tongue to its proper duty.

'At least tell me where I am,' he said in a much clearer voice.

'You are four kilometres from Essen,' the man explained gently. 'They are looking for you everywhere.'

'Haven't I just said that?'

'No, not your friends! The police! And Krupp's men. Herr Furst has been arrested and taken by train to Berlin to answer certain questions. The cab driver who dumped you here has fled. He has relatives in Duisburg. One way and another, things are not good for you.'

'Then I must thank you for harbouring me.'

'Is that what you think? We are waiting to see whether there is a reward for your capture.'

'You say Furst has been arrested?'

'Your partner in crime.'

'I need a doctor and a telegraph office.'

'And us? For the risk we are taking? What is there in that for us?'

If I could sit up, Philip thought. If I could look out of the cobwebbed window and see the lie of the land. The road, for example: Is it a highway or some benighted farm track? This is not a house but it is not a cow byre either. This man is not a farmer: What farmers wear is not what he has on.

He racked his brains furiously before it came to him. He was talking to a postman.

'I am not worth anything to you dead. You're a sensible fellow. There is money in this for you. Are you going to kill me for a watch and a pair of boots?'

'Maybe you die anyway.'

'No,' Philip said with terrible lassitude, his

99

eyelids quivering. 'If I was going to die of the gunshot wound I would already be dead. Listen to me. *Listen.*'

But whatever he was going to say floated away, like thistledown. He scrabbled feebly to find the man's hand, gave up and closed his eyes with an almost sensual abandon. For God's sake put some clothes on, Bella, he pleaded. You are acting as if it is Tuesday morning.

The postman's wife had joined her husband and stood watching Philip, arms folded. Unhappy marriage had turned her lips down at the edges and made her neck gaunt. She was insect-thin and breastless in a village of buxom and blustering neighbours but she had discovered a great truth in life. Once you are famous for never smiling, never deigning to look anyone in the eye, acting as though others did not exist, it is the easiest thing in the world to instil respect. Terror is a form of respect.

'What has he been talking about?' she asked. Her husband looked up at her.

'Gold,' he improvised. 'He wants a telegraph office.'

'Not here, for God's sake.'

'Of course not here.'

The woman thought about it, hugging her bony ribs. For something to do, she reached down and pulled the socks from Philip's feet, rolling them into a ball and stuffing them into the pocket of her pinafore.

'He can go to your brother,' she decided.

'The journey will kill him!'

'Hans-Georg can negotiate a price with London. He can do that for me.'

'For us,' her husband pointed out, without much hope of being listened to.

'Dig a trench,' she said. 'In case he does not recover in time to make the journey.'

'You want me to bury him?' the postman asked, amazed.

'What is *your* plan?' his wife retorted in her most cutting voice. 'Should we prop him up at the kitchen table?'

The postman's plan was to put him in a wheelbarrow and take Westland across the fields to the marshes and leave him to sink or swim. He had a horror of burying him in the garden. There was nothing religious about this. He was thinking of his neighbour's dogs.

'He isn't dead yet,' his wife said. 'Make him some soup.'

The postman seized his wife by her scrawny throat. It was not much of a marriage they had, but a man was a man.

'*You* make him some soup,' he commanded savagely and was rewarded by her mocking smile.

EIGHT

To her surprise—and a little to her irritation— Bella found herself increasingly taken with the hermit's conversation. What would have been tedious about Duxbury had she been trapped by him in a railway carriage or on some park bench was transformed by circumstance. Viewed from his cave, Yorkshire seemed huge, silent and invitingly empty. Reason told Bella that only two miles away

101

there existed a town, a castle, a railway station, the canal and the River Aire itself—but they were all as if spirited away by some giant hand. It was a giddy feeling.

The sun helped, making Bella feel warm and relaxed for the first time in days. When Alfie pointed out a kestrel circling high overhead, the three of them watched it with the same patience it showed in hunting out its prey. It was a long time since Bella had given anything in nature more attention than she did habitually to the printed page. She was saddened to see the bird move away over their heads to begin quartering the limestone bluff.

'You were saying,' she resumed drily.

For how the former tobacconist liked to talk, even going so far as to rise in the middle of an anecdote and walk to the edge of the cave to empty his bladder without so much as a breath to interrupt his story, the next elements of which he threw over his shoulder. The noisy splashing he made meanwhile shocked Alfie but amused Bella. She liked Duxbury for his cheery nonchalance, which he salted from time to time with the sort of prophetic remarks hermits are supposed to make.

'Take young Alfie here. He has a small fortune in ha'pennies and pennies he keeps under a floorboard in his room. When he has enough, he will leave his old mother and make his way to London. For there he has a mind to open a little shop and marry a pretty girl.'

'How did you know that?' Alfie asked, amazed.

'A little bird told me.'

'No, I mean about where I keep my savings?'

Bella could guess easily enough: from his

102

mother's several visits to see the hermit on other matters.

'And will he be happy when he is in London?' she asked.

'There will be setbacks,' the hermit said calmly. 'Selling sweeties is a difficult trade.'

'But how did you know it was going to be a sweetie shop?' Alfie yelped in anguish. Duxbury, who had sold a few hundredweight of sweeties in his day and had listened more than a few times to the boy's inventory of Minshall's stall on the market, gave Bella a sly glance.

What was to have been an hour's visit stretched into a day out. They made a round of Duxbury's rabbit traps (from one of which came his evening meal, despatched by Alfie) and listened to his unembarrassed prosing about Dame Nature, a lady who much resembled (one could say) a buxom apple-seller on Leeds Market. Alfie was a far more accurate guide to plants and insects, and his respect for the hermit was sorely tried on occasion; but the three dawdled the afternoon away in great content. Bella even found pleasure in watching Duxbury skin and quarter his rabbit.

Pressed by the hermit to stay and share the eating of it, she was torn between refusing and prolonging her visit to enjoy the late afternoon light washing the valley in watercolour tints. Moreover (she was forced to admit) for all his cheap theatrical effects and relentless jollity, there was something about the hermit she needed just as keenly as the credulous Alfie. After a few moments she accepted his invitation, on condition that Alfie returned to Skipton. She would follow in her own good time with the last hour of dusk to see her home.

'I am not happy with that,' the boy said.

'Then take the trap back and see to the mare, have a bite to eat yourself and then—if you must—come back on foot and I will meet you along the road. No harm shall come to me, Alfie, I promise.'

'What shall I tell the hotel?'

'You need tell them nothing. I am not a schoolgirl to be fussed over.'

Duxbury said goodbye to the disconsolate Alfie by ruffling his hair and patting him gently on the back.

'You can leave her safe with me, lad. I'll see to it she walks home before it comes full dark.'

'Y'ave talked all bloody day. What else is there to say to each other?'

'Well, I'll tell you next time I see you.'

'But Mr Sanderson has warned me to keep an eye on her.'

'Is that true?' Bella flashed. 'He used those exact words? Then be off with you right now, you impudent boy. And you may tell Mr Sanderson I shall not need your protection any longer, for I return to London tomorrow.'

Which was bluster of the worst kind, shaming enough to send her stomping out of the cave and heading towards the stream a hundred yards away, where Duxbury drew his water. Once there, she flung herself down onto a rock slab, her head in her hands. Her petulance was at full bore: had Alfie followed her down she would have brained him for certain—but when she looked round, he had gone. She calmed herself by taking off her boots and stockings and dabbling her feet in the water. It was cold enough to make her arteries jump.

Bella had an eye for nature, however uneducated it might be. By sitting still and letting her mind wander, she began to see more; and more deeply. Nor did Duxbury do anything, by a single word or gesture, to break this mood. When she looked back into the cave he was on his knees at the entrance, stewing the rabbit. Everything that was fanciful about him for the moment fell away. He was simply an elderly man who had to eat to live. It touched Bella that in a month, a year, five years hence, she might close her eyes at this time of day and imagine the hermit just as he was now.

She found herself thinking about the first time she and Philip had made love. That had taken place not in London but what had struck her at the time as the wilds of Shropshire. The same huge skies, the same unblinking indifference to human wishes. Set down in even the most commonplace of landscapes, how small she had seemed, how fatuous. She grimaced. For all his faults, the hermit had overcome something she did not like to admit in herself—a faint terror of nature. Trees could not love. Grass gave back nothing but stains. As if to punctuate these unhappy thoughts, a fly with brown mottled wings landed on the softer part of her bare calf and stung her painfully.

She walked into the stream with her skirts drawn up to her hips the better to dab water on the place, when something extraordinary caught her eye. Bobbing towards her was a paper boat, such as children make. It was broad enough in the beam not to have been capsized but with such plucky little ships things are usually undone so soon as they are waterlogged. This one showed no signs of foundering. It was only recently made.

Bella jumped out of the stream and scanned as far as she could see in every direction. Reason suggested she look for a child but her heart thumped out another possibility. She was being watched—and not by any adorable urchin. For a second or so her scalp crawled. Looked at in this new way, every shadowed fold or dip in the ground seemed malign. She sat down heavily and scrambled for her stockings.

And now is the time to get hold of yourself, she scolded, as clearly as if she had spoken these words aloud. If they have managed to get this close without being observed, you will not find them now—and even if you do, you are risking an arrow in your ribs. You are being toyed with: stay calm. For all they know, you are just another Skipton biddy come to see the hermit and this is their way of frightening you. But you are not frightened. You are their equal in brains and courage. You are Philip Westland's woman. He has not chosen a ninny to adore.

All the same, her defiance was not strong enough to make her call out or go and look for them. The idea of coming across two naked women and facing them down in a mutton-sleeved blouse and linen skirt was less than attractive. Quite right, a ghostly Philip agreed. Just this once, a lofty indifference is the better part. Perhaps a little insouciant whistling. I think moving back towards the cave could be seen as a mere tactical withdrawal, *reculer pour mieux sauter*. Scowling and scratching your insect bite is quite the wrong thing.

'I need to smoke,' she said aloud.

Duxbury was hymn-singing when she walked

back to the cave. Mad as he was, the sight of him poking about in his saucepan of stew was very reassuring. Bella found her bag and lit a cheroot, scanning the ground in front of the cave for signs of movement. It was all as peaceful as a churchyard. For all that, she felt jumpy.

Ursula Gollinge could not have made the paper boat; no one who spoke in such a clacking humourless voice, who was so positive of her own worth, would waste time folding paper. But Bella could imagine Amelia doing it. It was the difference between the petulant child who cannot hear how she sounds to others, who never listens to others, never looks out of the schoolroom window; and the sly companion she has designated as her best friend. And if so—if Amelia had sailed the boat towards her—maybe it was merely a joke, a spur-of-the-moment tease. Maybe, she forced herself to think, it was harmless.

'We shan't be long,' Duxbury promised, forcing her to turn her attention back to the cave interior.

'Do you entertain often?' she asked in the most casual tone possible.

'Never,' he murmured, without turning his head.

'The ladies from Cruddas never come to see you?'

'They do not and nor would they be welcome. Any more than the Bishop of Ripon and his lady. Hermits are picky folk.'

'I am your generous exception, then.'

Duxbury glanced up at her with an unsettling absence of levity.

'I asked you to stay on because you have something to say to me you could not speak of in front of the boy,' he pointed out, as if to a child.

Bella felt herself blush.

'I do want to talk. But the man I most want to talk to is not in the country at the moment. I think you know that.'

'It is written in your face. You are worried for his safety. And of course, you have a great decision to make.'

'And what might that be?'

'Why, whether to marry him,' Duxbury smiled.

'So now you are setting up as a consultant in marriage? Are you really the right person, I wonder?'

'None better. I was married at twenty and lived with the same woman for thirty-two years. We gave it a fair go together, buried all four parents, had two children of our own, watched them go the same road as us. And it came to me one day that I had seen nothing and understood nothing.'

'And since then you have been up here?'

'No better off to be sure,' Duxbury admitted. 'Only lonelier. Of course, my sad story will never happen to you.'

'Can you say why, hermit?'

'You ask too many questions for a start! You're a well set-up woman, a fine woman, no doubt about that, but in a general way you're as jumpy as a cat on hot cinders. It will take a bold man to tame you. Mebbe a desert sheikh might do it. Or an Indian prince, summat of that ilk. I speak frankly.'

'You speak as you find, as I have heard them say up here.'

'You don't recognise the picture I'm drawing?'

'That I'm jumpy? That may be so.'

'To be bold about it: you have come up here on a wild goose chase. You're not going to tell me

108

what, though I can guess. Today you had a good time of it and the frown went out of your face. Isn't that so?'

'I have enjoyed myself. You are a good host.'

'I am,' the hermit agreed calmly. 'And then all of a sudden you let yourself be trapped into saying you will go home on the morrow to spite a boy who has only half your brains.'

'I did not wish to spite him. The idea is ridiculous. I have things to do in London. Important things,' she blustered.

'I don't doubt. But what's in your mind right now is what brought you up here in the first place.'

'And do your powers extend to telling me what that is?'

'They do,' Duxbury said, pointing the stick he was using to stir the pot. But the gesture was far from comical. 'You want me to say the madwoman and her chit of a lover, o' course.'

'What about them?' Bella asked.

'Aye, what about them? Circus animals, I call 'em. But I don't think it's them that brought you up here. Not really. They were just the excuse to get you on a train and hop off out of things for a while.'

'You can't know that.'

'Can I not? The top and bottom of this whole jaunt, my dear, has been that you don't like who you are.'

Bella flinched. What the hermit said might be true but it was hard to take. Who does like who they are? Duxbury's remark was of the kind that she would have demolished in any salon in London but was not so easy to deny here, with his lined and filthy face turned towards her, not even the ghost

109

of a smile left on it.

'The reason is simple enough,' the hermit said.

Which is how she came to unburden her heart to a bundle of rags, while eating a rabbit stew she did not want and taking as her pudding a raw carrot he produced from a grimy paper sack. Duxbury was a good listener. Skipton was as far as he had ever travelled in his life but as she talked she sensed he could see and understand Orange Street and the intimacy it harboured. Alfie's idea of London was a fantasy and that was its appeal; but the hermit had the intuitive power the boy lacked. He did not see streets or buildings, but people. By her account of them, she saw that he recognised that Quigley would fail to understand him completely and that Billy Murch would find a way to use him, but the man he connected to most strongly was the mild-mannered and reclusive Charles Urmiston. Another shopkeeper, she thought hazily.

Like soldiers in their bivouac, they shared the last of Bella's cheroots. The hermit poked up the fire, for it was growing cold, and when she looked out of the cave's entrance, she saw that a vast mauve dusk had overtaken the valley.

'I must go,' she said.

'Aye and so you must.'

'I have said too much.'

Duxbury smiled and gently laid his blackened hand on her sleeve.

'You have told me nothing very much, widow-woman, and yet you have told me everything. The one gentleman you have not described in any detail is your friend Mr Westland. But were he to walk in here right now I should know him instantly, because of what you have told me about yourself.'

'Am I so very obvious?'

'I've told you about my marriage, haven't I? The kiddies and everything. *Their* kiddies. But the only time I ever understood another human being was with a man. His name was Franks. Nothing funny, if you take my meaning. We used to meet up once a week to play crib and sup ale. We did this for twenty or more years. I could get an idea of who he was just because he was another man, you understand. Married, like me. Ugly, like me. We got on famously.'

'What did you talk about?'

Duxbury laughed. 'We hardly said a word to each other in all that time. And certain-sure nothing deep. When he died, I saw that we had been made for each other. But he had to die first. People ask me what I miss about my old life. They mean armchairs and Sunday roast and the like. But the answer is Harry Franks. And you don't want to be going down that road.'

'Is there any hope for me, hermit?' she wailed.

'Tha'll do,' he murmured peaceably.

She bade him goodbye. It was by now dark enough to make the path back to the main road alarmingly hard to follow. What had seemed like a level walk in the morning was beset with rocks and unseen tussocks of grass that snatched at her feet. The safest way to navigate was to edge her way along the bluff, like someone feeling their way in a darkened room, their back to the wall. She was soon stranded on a narrow shelf that led nowhere and was forced to retrace her steps. To her dismay, she found herself walking downhill more than she remembered was necessary. Chilly though the night air was, she felt a trickle of sweat run down her ribs. She was lost.

The hand that closed over her mouth was warm and damp. The body that pressed against her back was unmistakably a woman's, soft and weighted in a way no man was fashioned. The low gurgling laugh in her ear belonged to the creature she had dreaded most to meet.

'Let me show you the way, my lovely,' Amelia whispered. And with that she threw her spare arm across Bella's stomach and ran her down a steep slope. Nothing could prevent them both from tumbling, which they did, rolling over and over. They fetched up in the beck, grunting like wrestlers, arms and legs flailing. Bella first had the breath knocked out of her and then her head hit a boulder. There was a flash as brief as lightning and the world disappeared.

*   *   *

'Mrs Bella Wallis, of 18 Orange Street,' Ursula Gollinge mocked. 'Such a very commonplace London address.'

'How do you know my name?'

'From your *carte de visite*. How thoughtful of you to carry it about. You need not feel your skull so tenderly. No skin has been broken.'

Bella looked about her. She was in what had once been a drawing room with plaster moulded ceilings and all the rest of what constituted eighteenth-century taste. A once-white marble fireplace, internal shutters to the long windows, an oak floor. This was a mine-owner's consolation prize to his wife for living so far from the Assembly Rooms in York, or the gathering of the gentry at

Norton Ferrers or Castle Howard. Those who had once sat in this room were the remote echo of such taste and refinement but not without determination. In the Yorkshire way of things, they were as good as anybody else and a great deal better than some. And then, gradually, time had overtaken the property. From being a proud statement of intent, the room had dwindled to what it was now. Which was not much better than a cow byre.

What furniture there was had been stacked recklessly at one end of the room, higgledy-piggledy. Table stood upon table, rugs and carpets were rolled or draped in the gaps between and—in Bella's eyes most wantonly of all—two hundred or so calf-bound books were scattered about like autumn leaves. By the side of the hearth, piled any which way, were boughs, lengths of sawn wood and several hundredweights of loose coal.

'What an eye for good living you have,' Bella commented. 'Never let anyone tell you pigs could do better.'

Ursula was wearing what she took at first to be a penitential sack but the colour—olive green—and the decoration—crow feathers and scraps of cloth—proposed another possibility. Lady Gollinge had dressed for the evening.

'You are pondering how and when to make a dash for it, Mrs Wallis. I strongly advise against that. Amelia is a dead shot with a bow. You wouldn't get very far.'

'People will be wondering where I am,' Bella warned.

'You think they will come looking for you with torches? What a vivid imagination you have. The

113

white man takes time to make up his mind.'

'You are yourself not white, of course.'

'I am white-skinned,' Lady Ursula allowed with magnificent hauteur. 'But there is an end to it.'

'And Amelia?'

'Is likewise gatekeeper to a better spiritual universe. Perhaps I should say a more real world.'

'You astonish me, Lady Gollinge,' Bella said with enough sarcasm to bring the ceiling down around their ears.

'I do not recognise myself in that title. The little fat woman in Windsor gave my husband a knighthood and then locked him in an asylum. All of that has nothing to do with me. People like you have nothing to do with me.'

'Then I wonder why I am here.'

'For my pleasure,' Ursula said. 'And to teach you something. Perhaps they will come here with torches. But only to ask whether I have come across any trace of you out on the moors. They don't like me but they have no reason to suspect me. The easiest explanation for your disappearance is that the earth has swallowed you up. Which is what I shall suggest.'

She leaned forward and stroked Bella's cheek with a grubby hand.

'How sad! You missed your way in the dark and fell into a disused mine. Which, when I have done with you, is just what will happen.'

'And what possible gain is there in that for you?'

'For me? None in particular. But the spirits who govern everything will be placated.'

'You are quite mad.'

'Do you know, I think I am,' Lady Gollinge said comfortably. 'There's great power in madness. The

114

earth shall be cleansed by it. You are here to be sacrificed, Mrs Bella Wallis of Orange Street in London. Something wonderful will happen to you at last.'

NINE

What struck Alfie most was the noise, the raw ripping and shredding of sulphurous air by shrieks and hoots, booming crashes and frantic clatter. There was no calm, no shelter—the cacophony seemed to run up and down the yellow walls like a lunatic. Perhaps a thousand people were bustling and shouting and the half-glimpsed roads and pavements beyond were black with others. It was raining hard and the gutters overflowed with filth. Immediately at Alfie's feet the water ran red: a cab horse had been pierced in the belly by a badly loaded dray and was on its knees, dying. Two men with hammers were trying to kill it stone dead by a blow to its head. A woman bystander sank to the pavement in a faint.

And the stink! Of soot and tobacco, fish and cabbages, horse piss and cooking fat, sweat and bay rum, wet cotton and rotting teeth! In the middle of it all, as if dumped there by capricious gods, an honour party of Guards in long grey coats and huge busbies, slow-marched a coffin draped in a Union flag towards a gun carriage. The officer in charge of the party carried a drawn sword. General Powicke-Elsom, who had stood his ground and served his Queen all these many years, was on the last leg of his journey from Quatre Bras to the

Guards Chapel. Welcome to King's Cross—welcome to the hub of Empire.

'Orange Street?' Alfie asked of a newspaper-seller sheltering under a canvas booth. The man jerked his chin by way of reply and the boy thought for a moment he was being given directions but all that was indicated was a policeman in a streaming tarpaulin cape.

'Now why would you want to go there?' this great man asked—Alfie's first taste of metropolitan condescension.

'Important message for a party.'

The policeman eyed him up and down in a leisurely way, wiping his moustaches by way of punctuation.

'Look like a drowned rat, you do.'

'Well, I aren't.'

'You're a lucky young sprout. And do you know for why? Wasn't I born in Bedford Street, which is not a thousand miles away from where you want?'

'Is it far?'

'Say an hour's brisk march,' the policeman said teasingly. Alfie merely nodded. Before this introduction to London he had formed no real idea of its size but the noise and confusion all around him indicated something huge, maybe a place as big as France, of which he had heard some details from Mr Sanderson. On the other hand, an hour's walk was nothing very much to a country boy and the policeman's jocularity fell flat. He was posted off down the Euston Road with a hearty shove in the back and instructions to bear left down Tottenham Court Road.

As Alfie squelched away, the constable straightened up and touched the brim of his helmet to a short and well-dressed man with a pale, unsmiling face.

'What is an hour's brisk march away?' Sergeant Tubney asked.

'Just a bit of fun with a country lad. A little gentle ragging to keep him up to snuff. The youth was asking after Orange Street.'

'Did he have luggage with him?'

'A cotton bag, slung over his shoulder, erm, on the right side if I recall.'

'Had he come out of the station?'

'Just popped up from nowhere. Swum up, if truth were known.'

'You called him a country boy.'

'Maybe a Yorkie. A Manc, maybe. Thick spoke, hard to understand. The way they rumble.'

'And a boy?'

'Wiry enough, but a boy, yes.'

'And why did he want to go to Orange Street?'

The policeman studied Tubney with just the tiniest flicker of fear in his eyes. Knew the bastard, a pushy cove if ever there was one and the scourge of the thieves and villains who worked the station. Attached to the Somers Town nick for the past month but never seen there. Had taken rooms for himself in Cartwright Gardens, if you please, as high and mighty as the Commissioner himself.

'Did you have an interest in the youth?' he temporised.

'Just answer the question.'

'Said he had a message to deliver.'

Tubney was already walking away.

*   *   *

117

'Well,' said Mrs Venn, pushing a strong cup of tea towards Alfie. Every stitch of clothing he had was hung on the backs of chairs in front of the open range. 'If this don't take the biscuit, coming in here like something fished out the Thames.'

'If I could have them clothes back—'

'Have them back! What, and have you die of cold right here in my kitchen? Hannah, my dear, give him another brisk-up with that towel.'

Hannah Bardsoe, who was visiting, beckoned Alfie to her.

'Come here, Carrot-top. And don't be shy about it. Me and Mrs Venn first seen what you've got to offer between your legs when we was blushing maidens ourselves.'

Unwillingly, Alfie gave up the towel round his waist and submitted to being buffed. Red as his skin was, his face was redder. Hannah kissed him absent-mindedly on his naked shoulder.

'Don't you worry. You're a good boy, I'm sure, and you're among friends. Cover your dignity and go sit near the range. And tell us your tale once again.'

It was five days since Bella's disappearance. The police had searched the house in Cruddas without result and though no one trusted Ursula Gollinge further than they could throw her, they were investigating her version of events: that this amiable London lady had called one night, having lost herself out on the moor. Had stayed for a meal and a bed and set off next morning with a view to inspecting the chapel at Ruthley before returning to Skipton. When the police investigated this location, they did in fact find a lady's bag. Empty, the way robbers leave bags.

118

'But you didn't believe this Gollinge creature, Alfie dear?'

'Not for a minute.'

'And for why?'

'Because there's nowt worth the seeing at the Ruthley chapel. It lacks a roof and is hardly bigger'n this here kitchen, just a pile of old stones. And more than that, I know Mrs Wallis. I have a fair idea of how she goes about things. They're lying.'

'They?'

'Gollinge and the lass 'Melia.'

'So then where is she, my mistress?' Dora Venn asked.

That was it, that was the reason why Alfie had prised up the floorboard in his bedroom and weighed out his hoard of coppers at the bank and taken the train to London. He did not believe she was dead or lost. He thought she was held captive somewhere by Ursula Gollinge, reasons unknown. There were details to his story that merely confused the two women: for example, Duxbury and Mr Sanderson. But the outline was clear. Something very nasty had happened to Bella.

'This Skipton place seems altogether a bit on the primitive side,' Dora Venn declared. 'I ain't ever been to Yorkshire but they don't seem to have their heads on the right way round. You have a few intelligent policemen up there, do you?'

'Out on the moors every day, additional sent for from Keighley. But the weather's turned, same as it has down here, and the search is going slow. Mr Sanderson thinks—'

'Yes, and is he the fat-arse one? He don't seem to have extended himself much—and him a man of the cloth.'

'What it is, Dora,' Hannah Bardsoe interrupted gently, 'this ain't going to be decided by the two of *us*. I'm wondering whether I shouldn't take this little ankle-biter back with me to meet my Charlie. Percy Quigley neither use nor ornament and in any case he ain't there, not at the present.'

'You think it needs a man's touch?'

'I do. *You* can't go nowhere, case she comes home. But Charlie might have an idea or two. He's very steady in this sort of situation.'

Mrs Venn passed Alfie his shirt and trousers and began pulling out the newspaper with which she had stuffed his very unsuitable boots. There was a point of etiquette here. She was Bella's servant and the meeting was taking place in her kitchen. It was for her to say what to do next, something Mrs Bardsoe understood only too well.

'We could run him round to that little chancer Tubney,' Dora suggested doubtfully. There was an eloquent silence, taken up in watching Alfie trying to get his strides on without making a peepshow of it. Then her common sense cut in.

'That's a very bad idea,' she admitted. 'I don't know what made me say it. Have your Charlie give the boy the once-over. But mind, Mrs B, I shall want to know what's decided.'

'Goes without saying,' Hannah agreed. 'He'll stop with us tonight and I'll be round in the morning with a full report.'

Which is how Alfie found himself walking up the Charing Cross Road, eating a toffee apple and being scolded to keep his feet out of the puddles by the good-natured Mrs Bardsoe. Neither of them noticed a sallow man with an impeccably tailored topcoat following after them, first on one side of the road, then the other.

* * *

'Well,' Charles Urmiston said in his usual quiet, kindly voice, 'I would say you have done exactly the right thing, Alfie. Mrs Wallis can be proud to count you as her friend. I don't suppose you saw into Lady Gollinge's house yourself? No, and how could you? But you think she might be hidden there?'

'They have her hid away somewhere for sure, the barmpots.'

'Yes, I can see your thinking there. But here's a thing. Why would they want to do that?'

Alfie had no answer. Urmiston picked up Hannah's plump little fist and bounced it gently on the chenille cloth covering the table.

'Mrs Bardsoe here is unshockable, Alfie. Between us, we have met some very rum characters out there in the shop, not all of them twenty shillings to the pound. And there have been others,' he added. 'Now, put your manners aside and tell us in what way these two women are a danger, as I take you to mean.'

'Anyone can see it.'

'Yes. But suppose you tell us what *you* have seen?'

When the story came out of hunting naked with bows and arrows, Alfie was surprised to find it was the gentleman who blushed and not Hannah. She grabbed the boy delightedly by the ears and wiggled his head from side to side, laughing at his description of sooty breasts and whitewashed

121

faces.

'If that don't merit the word "barmy", I don't know what does. It's as good as anything in any book I've ever read and that's no error!'

Charles Urmiston winced and when she realised what she had just said, Hannah did the same. Alfie misunderstood this exchange.

'I only looked at them a few times,' he said, hot in the face. 'Just to get at the cut of their jib—' snorting laughter from Hannah '—and Mrs Wallis saw them, same as me, the day before she disappeared. I think she knowed 'em from down here. Duxbury the hermit says she had come to see them special.'

'Duxbury the hermit,' Urmiston repeated faintly. He did not wish to be disloyal to Bella but what dearest Hannah had blurted out rang true. Henry Ellis Margam had stumbled into one of his own plots—perhaps it would be kinder to say into a story by one of his racier competitors.

'We can do nothing more today, Alfie. You will sleep here tonight. Mrs Bardsoe and I will debate what to do and in the morning we shall have a clear plan.'

'There is a particular gentleman Mrs Wallis is attached to,' Alfie pointed out.

'There is indeed. But Mr Westland is out of the country at the moment and cannot be reached. You will have to put your trust in me,' he added half-humorously.

Before bed, Alfie was give cocoa with an eggcupful of rum in it, which he counted the best thing that had ever passed his lips. Urmiston showed him to the attic, the room where he himself had started out in the house. He was bidden to sleep well and warned about the bottom step of the stairs, should he wish to visit the outside privy. It was easy to miss, as Urmiston could testify to by personal experience.

'You have seen little enough of London, you poor chap.'

'I shall come back one day.'

'One day soon, perhaps. We take breakfast at five. There is a good train to Leeds a little before seven. After that, I am in your hands.'

'And safe enough,' Alfie promised.

'Is it bad, Charlie?' Hannah whispered after they had all three gone to bed. Urmiston kissed her on her doughy cheek.

'Bella has survived worse. I would match her against most women in the given circumstances. But you know I shall have to take that boy back to Yorkshire tomorrow, dearest heart. I have no choice in the matter.'

'Could you not lay the whole thing before Billy Murch?'

'Would that I could! But time is of the essence here. We must travel by the first available train. And in any case—'

Hannah humped herself round in the bed and landed on him like the plumpest mermaid ever scrambling for a rock. Her kisses were hot and salty.

'Dear, dear boy! You think they care nothing of you! That you are not a man for a crisis. How foolish is that. You have their complete respect from top to bottom. For courage and wise counsel alike.'

'A petty shopkeeper,' Urmiston said bitterly.

'Ho! Well, as to that you can hang up your apron

any time that pleases you and go off to be a hero in more dangerous climes and among younger women, if that's how you see yourself. I never said you was a flashing blade or the best horseman in England. All that is for books, you great daftie.'

'Hannah—' he protested.

'I wouldn't trust you with anything bigger than an egg spoon, if it comes to that. But then again I wouldn't Mr Westland, neither. Petty shopkeeper! Well, if that don't beat all! The kindest, noblest—'

He kissed her, his free hand stroking her back, prickly tears in his eyes. It had long ago come to him that all he knew of women was to be found in the short library of Hannah Bardsoe's desires and passions. He loved her with an ache that hardly ever went away. When she said, as she often did, that they rubbed along well enough, he knew she was teasing him. Or, as she would put it, blowing fate a raspberry. Their kisses lengthened and she rolled him onto his hip.

'Be quiet, woman,' he whispered. 'I am planning my campaign.'

'Not tonight, Josephine,' she retorted, her hand reaching for him with a boisterousness that made him gasp.

*　　　*　　　*

Midnight in the Ruhr Valley, measured by the tolling of a church bell—not distant but located practically outside the window. Philip had been taken a journey to get to this room, flat on his back and covered in straw. Two men, or possibly one man talking to his horse, a bumpy ride that made thought impossible. Only tiny slivers of his transfer

124

from the postman's house remained intact as he slipped in and out of consciousness. Some sort of altercation with a cart passing in the opposite direction; later on, an attack by a determined dog. A woman's voice, the sound of geese being driven somewhere. A distant *train* passing.

Nevertheless, a good church bell and a bed to sleep in were decidedly steps in the right direction. Hock the wrong thing to order but possibly a glass of beer, were this a hotel. Which it resolutely refused to become. My name is Philip Westland and I am having the greatest trouble in getting the world to stand still for a moment or two.

'It is your liver,' Bella said in that absent-minded scolding tone she reserved for discussions about health. She was speaking from a balloon quite a way off, possibly with the help of a nautical speaking trumpet.

'The liver, eh?'

He spoke these words aloud and they caused a sudden stirring of shadows. There was a very large man in these new quarters called Hans Georg (not that he introduced himself) and his wife, or possibly his daughter, Anna. Hans Georg kept cows and understood enough of how to physic them to be able to dress a gunshot wound and reduce a fever. Philip was the better for a scalding poultice of what might have been horse radish and a pint of thin gruel. His naked body had been sponged by Anna with well-water so deliciously cold he could have wished her to continue with it all night long. Instead, she sat with her hair in a long plait reading the Bible, her finger following the lines of print. A single wavering candle lit the room.

125

'The thing to be remembered about Quigley—'
he mumbled. Anna looked up again.

'Yes, what about him?'

'I have forgotten.'

'Is this man your superior?'

'Which man?'

'Herr Quigley.'

'We quarrelled on the train back from Wiltshire.
Urmiston—'

'Yes, who is Urmiston?'

'Urmiston pushed me out of the carriage at
Basingstoke.'

She was writing all this down on loose sheets of
blue sugar paper. Philip reached out and touched
the tip of her breast with his fingers. She stopped
writing and sat very still. But unafraid.

'Where is the postman?' he asked.

'Franz? He is downstairs. You are still very
feverish.'

'If I close my eyes, everything is purple.'

'That is normal,' Anna said, as though she spoke
for consulting doctors Europe-wide. She took his
hand from her nightgown and laid it across his
belly. He felt lighter than a feather. And suddenly
very tearful.

'I need to telegraph London.'

'In the morning you can do this thing. But be
quiet now.'

'Who is that downstairs?'

'I have told you—Franz and my father. They are
playing cards.'

'Shall we make love?'

The German girl's laugh was pleasantly low and
intimate. She leaned over the bed and kissed him
briefly on the forehead.

'An excellent idea. But first we must ask Bella.'

Philip peered, confused.

'You know about Bella?'

'She has been mentioned,' Anna said with great dryness.

'She says that if you carry a gun, you are more likely to be shot by a gun. Which is absolute nonsense.'

'I think so,' Anna agreed. 'But Bella is beautiful, no?'

Philip embarrassed them both by bursting into tears. Downstairs—but where downstairs?—there was the scrape of a chair being dragged back across stone flags. The noise gave an unmistakable indication of sudden exasperation. Then came heavy boots clumping on the stairs. Fee fie foe fum.

Hans Georg was certainly the height of the door but also half its width. At some point in the evening he had taken off his shirt, leaving a black forest of hair that ran from his gut, to gather under his chin and there form the undercroft of an impressive beard. In his hand he held a short-handled mallet with an iron head.

'Why don't I kill you, English? This fever you have, you hold onto like an old woman. Oh, look at me, oh, boo-hoo. Better I kill you.'

'Where is the profit in that?' Philip asked conversationally, as though discussing leading out trumps from a weak hand.

'Tonight comes a captain of police from Essen, yes, from Essen. Saying how much they would like to interview you. There is a man with him, a Berliner.'

'What did he have to say?'

'He don't say nothing. But before he sits down, he wipes the chair with his handkerchief. Eh?'

'You paint a very clear picture.'

'He doesn't know what he is saying,' Anna warned. 'He is burning up with fever.'

'He knows,' Hans Georg muttered. 'Why should we fool with the police? Now, if it all comes out, I got problems with this captain, an ugly bastard with a silly fucking beard.'

'Some beards are beautiful,' Philip protested.

'You shut your face. Tomorrow we telegraph London.'

'Excellent.'

'I give your representative three days to get here. With a hundred gold sovereigns.'

'You flatter me.'

'Tonight Anna stays with you.'

'Not necessary. Very generous, but quite the wrong thing. Too kind.'

Hans Georg looked at him with fury.

'To stop you from running away.'

Fever or not, Philip thought this was the funniest thing he had ever heard. Snorting laughter, helpless beating of fists on the mattress, a threatening looseness in the gut, general mild delirium.

'Bring him more blankets.'

'Maybe a mattress?' Anna suggested.

'Good! And you, you fool: do you hear me? No more laughing! We sweat you like a horse, then you are better.'

Philip's whinny came near to extinguishing the candle.

TEN

Urmiston arrived at Skipton dressed in Hannah Bardsoe's idea of an outfit appropriate for the distant parts of the kingdom. His ginger wool shooting jacket was belted and had leather shoulder patches. No power on earth could have persuaded him to wear the breeks that went with this garment: Hannah knew that and had substituted a pair of corduroy trousers in duckpond green. Urmiston had big feet and these were encased in alpine climbing boots with metal clips to guide the laces. On his head he wore a soft tweed cap. All these things were second-hand and had been assembled by Hannah from clothes stalls over the last year or so against the day when her beloved Charlie would be recalled to the colours, so to speak. At King's Cross they had seemed woundingly eccentric but here in Skipton they passed without comment. A long nose and lantern jaw helped.

'Good day, maister,' the ticket collector at the station said, without the slightest suspicion of irony.

'He thinks you're somebody important,' Alfie whispered.

'Which of course I am. Now cut along and see your mother and we shall meet again at, say, two this afternoon.'

'Where?'

'At the George, I think.'

'Shall I walk you there now?'

'I doubt it is hard to find.'

129

They parted and Charles Urmiston walked into town, very conscious of being the representative of a loose-knit circle of London friends that had but one thing in common—their loyalty to a grey-eyed widow who had come to Skipton and somehow overreached herself. In all other respects, they were a most unlikely band of brothers. Among them, Urmiston counted himself the least.

As it happened (for all his weird and wonderful costume) he alone could be placed as a possible social acquaintance of Bella's, say a bookseller friend ruined by failure or a distant cousin driven mad by the study of Aramaic in some forsaken vicarage. He was, in the modest way of it, a gentleman. But how to explain—even under the elastic notion of six degrees of separation—Percy Quigley's quirky adhesion to Bella's cause? How to introduce the implacable Billy Murch as another of Bella's friends to this file of schoolchildren in pinafores being marched back into school?

It was Urmiston's habit to sell himself short. The truth was, he knew more of provincial England than any of the friends who gathered under Bella's banner. His work as a land agent to three successive railway companies had certainly taught him how to deal with bumptious local upstarts.

'I must warn you that gentlemen generally dress for dinner in this hotel,' the insolent day manager of the George murmured, having seen his clothes and cast a supercilious eye over his luggage, a single portmanteau. Urmiston stared him down.

'I do not like to be warned,' he said. 'The word you were searching for in this instance was "advise", I am sure.'

130

'One way or another, you won't be admitted to dinner in those clothes.'

'I see.'

Urmiston pulled a sheet of the hotel's writing paper from a wooden rack and studied it briefly. Something in the heading caught his eye and made him burst out laughing. 'Well, well,' he exclaimed. 'From this we understand the proprietor of the hotel to be Mr Herbert Lintott. Go and fetch him at once.'

'I cannot leave my post.'

Urmiston rounded on a cowering potboy in a red and silver striped livery waistcoat.

'Go to Mr Lintott's office and ask him to step along to the front desk. He will want to know why. Tell him you have been sent by Mr Charles Urmiston. Remind him the last time he met Mr Urmiston was in Swindon, when he had the Perceval Hotel. Go on, child. Skip away.'

The day manager could not be sure this ploy was genuine but prepared himself for the possibility that it was.

'I was merely pointing out to the gentleman—'

'Is that the residents' lounge? Ask Mr Lintott to join me there.'

Bravado was one of life's rich pleasures. He had almost forgotten how intoxicating it could be.

*   *   *

'My dear old Charles!' Bert Lintott chuckled, over and over. 'If this don't beat all. My word, I am so delighted to see you. And look, let's get the sad news out of the way first: my commiserations about the loss of your wife. Mary took it most feelingly.

131

We wrote to the house in Campden Hill—'

'A lot had changed by then, Bert. We had fallen from grace somewhat—'

But he was sure Lintott already knew that. The hotelier would have followed the disgrace and dismissal Urmiston had suffered at the hands of the Great Western Railway as a matter of professional interest. That they were friends went without saying; but that all friendship was a matter of checks and balances was also understood. These two first knew each other in the days of Urmiston's pomp, when he was a highly respected servant of the railway company and Lintott as unctuous as any Yorkshireman ever wishes to be when among the condescending baboons that run the country to the south. Urmiston knew too that his old friend could price his travelling outfit to the last shilling—and in it, read his present fortune.

'You finally kept your promise to Mary,' he suggested, waving his arm to indicate not just the lounge but the whole hotel—and indeed the town.

'It was always what she wanted,' Lintott boomed. 'Be damned with all this, mind, but she said to me one day, "Bertie, I want you to take me back to Yorkshire and buy me that little white house on the road to Grassington, the one we used to gawp at when we were courting." Captain Shelley's house, as was. So we came up here for a poke about and blow me, Charles, if it wasn't on the market and just as we remembered it. As neat and comely as any house ever built. The hotel was an afterthought. A partnership,' he added primly. 'There's four of us own it.'

'Nobody could wish you more joy than me, dear old lad.'

'And I think you mean that,' the Yorkshireman said, wiping his eyes with a pass of his meaty wrist. Urmiston smiled his gentle smile.

'I do—and while we're at it, let's get something else out of the way. I haven't come up here to play the old soldier with you, as I think is the expression. You are looking at a solid citizen in good standing with his community. I live with a respectable widow and together we run a little herbalist's. I have never been happier.'

'In London, is it?'

'Oh, yes, but in such a London as you and I grew up knowing nothing of. Well, of course,' Urmiston added hastily, 'I must speak for myself there.'

Bert Lintott laughed and stroked his friend's sleeve with a very affectionate caress. 'By shots, but it is such a pleasure to see you again, old lad. Tell me, how did you know I was here?'

'Five minutes ago, I didn't. I came up here to look for a guest of yours.'

'Mrs Wallis,' the hotelier said at once in a changed voice. The smiles and laughs had disappeared. He and his entire staff had been interviewed by the police the previous day. Mrs Wallis might be a very nice woman but her disappearance was business.

'A very dear friend,' Urmiston explained artlessly.

'Is it a particular *kind* of very dear friend we're speaking of?' Lintott enquired cautiously. He was relieved by Urmiston's hearty laugh.

'She is just that, but not in the sense you mean. Good Lord, my Hannah would dot your eye for thinking so. No, she is a fine impetuous woman who may have got herself into bother.'

133

'You can say that again,' Lintott growled. 'I come straight to the point as always. Do you know about the cuckoos we have up at Cruddas?'

'A very bright boy called Alfie Stannard has given me the general background, yes.'

'Well, there you are. If those two women haven't a hand in it somewhere, I shall eat my hat.' But behind the bluster, Urmiston thought he heard a more sombre note. Lintott was repeating taproom gossip by way of preparing his friend for something worse.

'There has also been mention of the hermit Duxbury.'

The Yorkshireman slapped his thigh in irritation.

'This is a hard-working market town. In the ordinary course of things we would have as much use for the woman Gollinge and that fool of a hermit as a chocolate teapot. But they have suddenly become meat and drink to the local press, as if the place had become a nest of witches. None of it helps find Mrs Wallis.'

'Has Lady Gollinge spoken to the press, then, to put herself under such suspicion?'

'She has fired a dozen or more arrows at them and that's better than an interview.'

'And the police?'

'Searched the house and found nothing. Which proves nothing.'

'You are angry, Bert.'

'I am better than angry. Gollinge and her impudent chit of a companion have made us a laughing stock. Which suits her, for she will never have a better stage to play on. She has found a printer—Rawson, the great fool—to publish her

134

insane theories about hunting and gathering and all the rest of the tosh she talks.'

'A pamphlet of some kind?'

'Being set up in type right at this moment. And according to Rawson, the first edition already sold out by subscription.'

'Maybe I should start with this hermit fellow.'

'Ha! According to the locals, you'll find him struck dumb by the same mysterious power that abducted Mrs Wallis,' the hotelier said in disgust. 'A brisk kick up the arse is what these people need.'

'Will you tell me what you really think, Bert? As a friend?'

Lintott stirred uneasily. Always a touching sort of a man, he reached across and seized Urmiston's hands in his two meaty paws.

'The moors are a dangerous place for the foolhardy. I fear for your friend, old lad. There are pits out there that are no more than twenty feet deep but twenty feet is plenty when you fall down one. The bigger workings would swallow a regiment. The whole town would like it to be voodoo or devil worship that's taken her, but it could be something simpler.'

'That she fell down a mine shaft?'

'They have no proper headings, do you see? There's nothing much to give warning, even in full daylight. There are parts where I wouldn't walk or picnic—and I was born here.'

'Then we might never find her,' Urmiston guessed, his eyes prickling.

'Has she anything of the countrywoman about her?'

'She is as London as Westminster Bridge,' he

135

answered brokenly.

'No, but let's see some more fight in you, Charlie,' Lintott said, alarmed by these tears. 'That bloody fool Duxbury was the last to speak to her before her disappearance, I believe. Since when nothing and no one can get him to utter. You must start there. He might just know something. And let it be a flying kick up the arse you give *him*, Charles. You have the boots for it.'

*   *   *

Alfie showed him the way. The boy was against using violence towards the hermit, though he knew in his heart it would never be offered. Urmiston had already impressed him by retrieving a magpie's feather and setting it upright in the turf. It was something local children were taught to do by their grandparents. That sat well with Alfie. The Londoner also stopped more than once to get the lay of the land, a thing practically unheard of among townies. Lastly, he seemed abstracted, as he had been for the whole train journey north. A puff of wind might blow him away, Alfie judged with the cruelty of the healthy young, but a deep thinker all the same. A bit of a brain-box, even. All the same he was completely taken aback when Urmiston asked him an unexpected question.

'You mentioned Mr Duxbury burying the bones of Raybould the murderer. Now where was that, exactly?'

'Turned him into a waterfall, he did.'

'Mmm. Would it be down there, at all?' Urmiston asked, pointing.

'I have never seen it.'

136

'Well, this is how it is, Alfie. We shall divide our forces. While I talk to the hermit, you shall scout for the place. But quietly and perhaps I should say secretly. So as not to tip our hand to prying eyes.'

'I can do that.'

'Good boy. When you have found it—'

'Mother has invited you to sup with us tonight, I forgot to say—'

'And I look forward to it. When you find the grave—or waterfall—come and fetch me. And now I think I see the hermit's smoke.'

'Is it important, about Raybould?'

'That is what we must find out.'

'You won't forget Mother's invitation?'

'No elephant has a better memory. Now be off with you.'

And watched with some envy as the boy ran straight down the side of the valley, as easily as if it had been Long Acre on a quiet Sunday. Like Bella before him, Urmiston was a little overwhelmed by the huge skies and empty spaces.

When he entered Duxbury's cave, he disconcerted the hermit by sitting down and saying nothing at all, not so much as a murmur of greeting. The two sat facing each other across a smoky fire. Urmiston had never met a hermit but—at the lowest point of his life—had known several deeply disturbed human beings. Only one or two were dangerous. For the most part, like Duxbury, they were losers with a gift for self-delusion. He was, accordingly, prepared to wait. A full five minutes passed.

'The Queen has lost her silver thimble,' the hermit said suddenly. 'All the ladies of the Court are looking for it.'

'Her Majesty enjoys these little games,' Urmiston responded gravely. 'The thimble is not lost but hidden. But I think you know that, for I have been told you are a very wise man.'

'Then where is the thing now?'

'That is what I am here to ask.'

Duxbury studied the fire of gorse twigs and rabbit dung for a while and then shrugged out a short smile.

'You are a friend of Mrs Wallis.'

'That is so.'

'Are you the one they call Urmiston?'

'Now that *is* very clever. She has told you about me, to be sure, but only a gifted man could have made the connection. Yes, I am Charles Urmiston. I have come to bring her home.'

'I cannot help. You are too late for that, I reckon.'

But Urmiston was ready for this answer; had anticipated it. Never a bold man, but not a complete ninny either. And he sensed that Duxbury was on the back foot. He played a weak card strongly.

'Hermit, I do not wish to threaten you but if I must I will go to the police and tell them how you poisoned Mrs Wallis with these pills that I recovered from your cave.'

He held out a tiny brown bottle of Bardsoe's Imperial Cough Lozenges, manufactured by him at the herbalist's in Shelton Street and slipped into his pocket by Hannah Bardsoe to ward off any chestiness that might be about in Yorkshire.

'There could be anything in that bottle,' Duxbury scoffed.

'Mrs Wallis told you about my little shop? Four

138

of these, mashed up with a few biscuits, will kill a dozen rats. You have heard of arsenic, I don't doubt?'

'The police will never believe you. They will want to have them examined.'

'You don't think it would work?'

'We may seem slow to Londoners but we are not daft.'

'Then I must try another tack. But be sure about something, Mr Duxbury. The police are very anxious to arrest someone and you are my candidate.'

'I never harmed a hair on her head.'

'But you were the last person to see her. You kept her back when Alfie Stannard went home and I think you know what happened after she left.'

'It was dark. She lost her way. Everybody thinks that. How should I know different?'

'Because you are a wise man. Would I come out here at all unless I believed in your powers?'

'Very well, then. She was taken by the girl Amelia,' Duxbury said without bothering to conceal a crooked smile at his visitor's reaction. 'You don't know whether to believe me, do you?'

'If you say it is so, it is so,' Urmiston said uneasily.

'I have never knowingly told an outright lie,' the hermit asserted far too grandly.

'Now this is better. Thank you for that. But you see, I still have a little problem that you can help me with. You liked Mrs Wallis?'

'As much as I knew of her.'

'Of course you did. I have never known anyone take against her on first acquaintance, as we might say. She paid you the respect due to you?'

139

'Enough,' Duxbury allowed.

'Yes. Quite so. A lady from London spends the day with you and accepts your kind offer of hospitality. After she has left, you see—or hear—her abduction and can identify the young companion of Lady Gollinge as her abductor.'

'Where's the problem with that?'

Urmiston rubbed the smoke out of his eyes. He examined his hands as though discovering them for the first time in his life. Sighed.

'I am not one of Mrs Wallis's bolder or braver friends. In many areas of life I am considered a bit slow on the uptake, even. But I do like an orderly story, Mr Duxbury. So here's my problem. Why did you not report these goings-on to the police? Oh, I know you have your dignity as a hermit to uphold and ideally the world should come to you. I see that very clearly. But then, next day, the police *did* come to you. And, bless me, you had nothing to say! In fact, you would not utter a single word.'

'It is none of my business. Let them work it out for themselves. The Gollinge woman is the chief suspect, if they have eyes to see.'

'Mmm.'

Alfie appeared all in a rush at the cave's entrance and Urmiston smiled and held his finger to his lips.

'I'm just getting it completely straight in my mind, hermit. On that strange night, Mrs Wallis leaves. A little later Alfie here arrives all of a fluster, just as he is now. She has not reached the road to Skipton. She might be lost on the moors. You say nothing. You know what has happened and you say nothing.'

'He put his finger to his lips, same as you just

140

done,' Alfie piped.

'An important detail. You asked him to tell you what had happened and what did he do?'

'Pushed me out of the cave.'

'What did he say when he did that, Alfie?'

'Was struck dumb. They had laid a curse on him.'

'Bless me! A curse! Why hadn't I thought of that for myself?'

'Sarcasm now, is it?' Duxbury blustered.

'Alfie admires you, Mr Duxbury. He thinks you are a deep cove. And so perhaps you are. I think it very likely that Lady Gollinge *did* lay a curse on you. Not the night of Mrs Wallis's disappearance but somewhat earlier.'

'More riddles.'

'Maybe so. I am going from here to the waterfall you made of Raybould's bones. Raybould the farmer, who knew these moors as well as any man that lived, I daresay. And yet the poor fellow dies crossing a stream. A heart attack, possibly. So severe that he cannot as much as drag himself to the far bank. Tragic.'

'Who *are* you?' Duxbury whispered.

'A small shopkeeper like yourself. And like you, not a complete fool. So here's the thing. You find the man all Skipton has been looking for for twenty years or more and you say nothing. You tell no one in authority. Some hermits keep a vow of silence, I know. But you are not such a one. As Alfie said on the way here, in normal times you talk fit to turn a mill.'

'You can clear off out it now,' the hermit decided.

'In a moment. But first, shall I tell you what I

141

think? That either you witnessed who killed poor Raybould, or you did it yourself. And now I shall leave, just as you ask. I shall go to where you buried him and keep a guard on the place. Alfie meanwhile will go back into Skipton and fetch the most senior policeman he can find. And then we shall all be a bit further down the road to the truth.'

'I did not kill him.'

'We shall need a senior policeman, Alfie, and a good doctor.'

'I had nothing to do with it,' Duxbury cried.

'Then I advise you not to bolt. One way or another, this is the second crime you have concealed, hermit, and it will go better with you if you don't dress up the facts with nonsense.'

*   *   *

Some of the smaller bones from Raybould's skeleton had washed into the pool below the waterfall. Urmiston found himself unable to touch them: they lay a few inches down on a bed of gravel. As to the stones piled on the rest of the farmer's mortal remains, he felt almost a religious inhibition from moving even one. Nor was there any need. Time and the brutal indifference of nature had laid bare all the evidence a man might want. Raybould's skull, which once had been the seat of such almighty remorse, was now a cistern. Luckily for Urmiston's stomach, only the back of the skull was visible, as an unmistakable round of bone. A ragged hole the size of a penny ruined its symmetry. Through that hole dribbled a brown thread of peaty water. In summer dribbled. In winter spouted.

*   *   *

'However did you work it all out, sir?' Mrs Stannard asked.

'To say I worked it out is some exaggeration,' Urmiston smiled weakly. 'It was a nagging detail. Mr Duxbury is a mighty fantasist and I could not believe the waterfall story, except as an example of his rather feeble whimsy. But, as we passed through Wakefield in the train this morning, it occurred to me to ask: What if he was telling the truth? Wasn't there mischief in that? Mischief of some kind?'

'Another baked apple,' Alfie's mother proposed, filling his plate before he had time to answer. 'I will tell you straight, sir, you have done more in one afternoon than the police have managed over five days. The lady was a special friend of yours?'

'Is, Mrs Stannard. Is.'

'Just as you say, sir. I don't know what came over me to speak so careless. I put Alfie at your complete disposal, Mr Urmiston, for all that is left to do. A good boy and as for common sense, well, he has his moments. Not a great scholar—'

'He has already proved his worth in far more practical ways—'

'Which I thank you for saying. Yes, indeed, praise from you is worth the having. We shall soon see an arrest, I am sure; and if my Alfie can be of the slightest help to you in the meanwhile, you have but to ask.'

'With Mr Duxbury in police custody and shaken free of the curse laid on his tongue I think it likely

143

that Lady Gollinge will join him at the station first light tomorrow. And then perhaps Bella—Mrs Wallis—will be found safe and well.'

'May the Good Lord make it so.'

'Amen to that,' Urmiston answered dutifully.

ELEVEN

A dozen stubs of candles were spread across the floor, their flames bending and trembling to the only movement in the room. Amelia was dancing. Her naked body glistening, her hair tied in a towering topknot, she swooped and spun, her limbs making fantastic shadows. When she stamped her feet, ancient dust jumped out of the floorboards in percussive grey lines. This imitation of something ancient and primal in a ruined Yorkshire house had completely erased the girl she actually was, or had been before Ursula found her. She was not tranced but neither was she in the slightest way that other Amelia who once had loaded and unloaded barges along the Liverpool to Leeds canal. Whatever was ribald and feckless about *that* creature had vanished. The dance had taken over.

Written down, Bella thought deliriously, all this would seem preposterous in the extreme. As it was, tied to a chair by her wrists and ankles, she watched the whirling body with something like terror in her heart. The room was insufferably hot. Behind her back, Ursula Gollinge drummed and chanted four notes over and over in a jagged corncrake voice. Bella felt her head falling into the

144

same hypnotic rhythm. Against the wishes of her rational mind, she was as if nodding agreement to the thick air, the leaping shadows, the invocation of all that was dark and mysterious.

And then it was done. The candles were stamped out one by one, the drumming fell to a whisper, followed by a piteous shriek from the girl; and silence. One instance of how powerful the experience had been was that when Bella tried to gather her wits, she could not say for sure whether the others were any longer in the room or not. She slumped in the chair, her mind reeling, her clothes damp with sweat.

This is nothing, Philip said to her from a long way away. His tone was gently chiding, the way he sometimes spoke to her upon the pillow. You are not harmed, dearest Bella. It is more likely that the poor deluded Lady Gollinge will mend her ways and take up embroidery long, long before you bend the knee to an exhibition of such cheap magic. Wipe all this nonsense clean. Find your centre. For example, taking the drawing-room mantelpiece in Orange Street, identify the objects on it from left to right. Name three admirals of your acquaintance. What is the sum of fifty-two and seventeen?

'Are there spirits in the world?' Ursula Gollinge interrupted unexpectedly from the far end of the room. 'Is there a world of spirits, the least parts of which are more powerful than any temporal king or emperor?'

Bella blinked, the sweat from her hair running into her eyes. She found the salty sting reviving.

'Can we have some light?'

'Are you afraid of the dark?' the lulling whisper

145

continued. 'Tonight it teems with spirits. Your father is here, for example.'

'I doubt it. He is rather fussy about the people he is seen dead with.'

'You should be much more afraid than that,' Ursula warned angrily.

'I am sorry not to oblige you. Standing on the roof of Westminster Abbey would fill me with terror. But not the gutters where your imagination lives.'

Well said, the ethereal Philip murmured, but with a more doubtful tone to his voice than she would have liked. Remember, we are not here to insult her but to escape. Bella chewed her lower lip, vexed. He made escaping sound like walking down a short flight of steps towards a waiting cab. But having pledged herself to stand and fight, there could be no turning back. Even when tied to a chair, she reflected groggily.

'Your inspiration for all this nonsense is the time you spent among the Australian aboriginals, I take it. What happened to your German, by the way? Perhaps he was of a more rationalistic turn of mind. Or less gullible, as we might put it.'

'What do you know of him? Who told you about him?'

'Try not to appear indignant, Lady Ursula. The poor man is an important part of your myth. He died nobly, I suppose. Is there some rock sacred to his name in the lonely outback? Is his memory kept alive in song and dance? Was he here tonight?'

Ursula Gollinge walked out of the shadows on stiff legs and struck Bella's face with the flat of her hand, as hard as she knew how.

'You think you are better than me?'

'Saner,' Bella replied, feeling blood in her mouth. The taste was strangely invigorating.

'How could you understand what you have just seen, a complacent white woman such as you are?' Ursula demanded.

'Ah, yes. That again. *Was* your German noble, or did he plead with you to stop these foolish games and return to Melbourne where there were medicines and feather beds, white wine and all the other wicked contrivances of the imperialist master race? Was he a disappointing German in the end?'

'He was torn apart by wild dogs.'

'I am sorry to hear it.'

Something of the evening had wrought its magic, nevertheless. Bella had the clearest image of an emaciated young man being tossed to and fro by dogs in some stony gully under a pitiless sun. Imagination provided his leather satchel and silver repeater and all the other rags of his previous existence. In spite of herself, she shuddered.

'He came close to the mystery but it eluded him,' Ursula explained dreamily.

'The *mystery*? My God, what utter piffle you talk when you are excited, Lady Gollinge.'

'He was my husband.'

'You already had a husband.'

'My husband under the stars.'

'For as long as it lasted. Was it worth it?'

Having her face caressed was worse than being struck. Ursula stroked her throat and jaw almost absent-mindedly, as another woman might smooth laundry.

'You don't have to understand a thing to know it is beautiful. You want me to say I understood nothing of what happened to me among the Aborigines and perhaps you are right. In your own mean-spirited way you are right. But I was given something you will never have.'

'And what might that be?'

'Why bother to explain? You could not begin to understand.'

'Are the Aboriginals a peaceable people?'

'They wish only to be left alone.'

'Your arrival must have been doubly vexing therefore. Two foolish Europeans, neither of whom could think straight for more than half a minute at a time.'

To say that Ursula laughed was to understate the noise that came from her—a wild howling bellow that fanned Bella's face. Bella felt her flesh creep. Then this, disgusting and unexpected: while her hands bore down on her captive's pinioned forearms, Ursula Gollinge spat full in her face.

'A curse on you and your kind!' she whispered. 'I call on powers that will shrivel you to dust!'

Amelia re-entered the room, dressed in a white shift, her face scrubbed clean of sweat, her hair undone. She went immediately to Bella's chair, pushed her mistress out of the way and began untying the ropes that held their captive there. It was an electrifying shift in authority.

'Go and fetch us to drink,' the barge girl commanded. 'You've said enough for one night.'

To Bella's amazement, the older woman filed obediently out of the room.

'Don't try nothing,' Amelia warned, as the last knot came undone. Bella chafed her wrists and plucked at her clothes, shaking like an aspen.

'How much longer can this go on, Amelia?'

'Until they catch us.'

'Are you not worth more?'

'You would know, of course,' the girl scoffed. 'I went on the barges when I was ten years old. I'm seventeen now. What would you have me do? Go back to shovelling spuds from out the hold or unloading forty tons of pig iron in some snowstorm? I'll take no lectures, thank you very much.'

'Your companion is heading straight for an asylum, you can see that, can't you? Does it have to end like that for you too?'

'I can look after myself.'

'And the police?'

'What of them? I can outrun any man set down on earth. And best of all, disappear when it comes to that, just vanish, pfft. Maybe she *wants* to be caught so's to kick up more dust. But not me. They can look as far as Timbuktu, they'll never find me. I'll run through mirrors first.'

All this with great good humour, as though explaining what was obvious. She pulled Bella up by her wrists and led her to the fire.

'She plans to kill you,' Amelia said. 'There are shafts round here that you can chuck a pebble in and never hear it strike. And you're right, she has bats in her belfry more than enough. But that's how it's worked out, like.'

'And that doesn't frighten you?'

'It's a laugh,' Amelia said, with the staggering cruelty of the half-formed.

'A *laugh*?'

'I don't say you would find it funny. But then you're not me, are ya? She's told me a lot about you, Mrs Bella Wallis.'

149

'Before all this, she had never met me. She has deceived you.'

'Happen so. But she goes on about you something cruel. So, do you want to be chucked down a lead mine?'

'It would take two of you and all your strength,' Bella blustered.

'Aye. Two of us,' the barge girl said with a derisive smile. 'So best keep in my good books, London woman. Can you hear what's outside?'

'I hear nothing.'

'You don't hear the dogs of Cruddas barking?'

*   *   *

Urmiston had been entirely correct in supposing the police would try to storm the Gollinge manor house but wrong as to timing. He had imagined a dawn raid but bargained without the confusion of having two police forces represented. After heated exchanges under the canopy of the Skipton railway station, twenty officers from two forces had been assembled and marched in column up the road to Cruddas, their boots cracking out a fine rhythm, while advertising their presence to every living thing. The dogs Amelia heard barking were responding to this heavy crunch-crunch up the hill to Cruddas: they had never known of such a thing and were more fearful than indignant. The fool of a farmer who added to the midnight confusion by letting off a twelve-bore from the gates to his midden saved Bella's life. The police fled into ditches, cursing and shouting. For an hour there were whistles and shotgun blasts, wild orders and the barking of chained dogs enough to beat the

150

band. When the first constables arrived at Lady Gollinge's house, soaked to the skin and in a filthy temper, they found it deserted.

All of which Charles Urmiston witnessed, having been dragged from sleep by Alfie. The two of them followed the police up to the village in drenching rain and though told to turn back, managed to stumble their way by roundabout route to the assault on the manor house itself. Much shouting and banging, the flitting of lanterns and exasperated cursing.

'They've bunked off out of it,' Alfie whispered.

'Perhaps only as far as one of the outhouses.'

'No. She's too canny for that, is Amelia. They've gone.'

The elm they sheltered under gave some relief from the weather but both Urmiston and the boy were drenched to the skin. Alfie watched as his new hero took out a moleskin purse (pressed on him by Hannah) and poked about inside. His fingers found one waterlogged banknote and a handful of coins. Urmiston dragged Alfie up by his wrist.

'Now we run—*run,* Alfie—to what used to be Captain Shelley's house along the Grassington Road. Do you think you can find it?'

' 'Tis two miles in the wrong direction!'

'It can't be helped. I have a friend there—'

'Mr Lintott—'

'Yes, Mr Lintott, who can fit us out with fresh duds and the loan of some money. For this could turn out to be a long search.'

'Mr Urmiston, sir, we have no time for that. The ladies have no more than half an hour's start. Running downhill to start with, for how else would

151

you put distance between yourself and trouble? But by the time we've done with Mr Lintott and all such, who's to say where they'll be? We have to go *now*.'

They might have argued more but for a shout from the courtyard of the house and some excited pointing in their direction. This might have been the time to help the police with their inquiries, Urmiston reasoned. Instead, hand in hand with Alfie, he tobogganed down a muddy slope on his back and once upright, began running like a man trying to escape a dozen maddened bulls. A very small and inadequate moon lit the way.

* * *

Philip Westland woke to find the fever had left him. In its place was a draughty clarity, as though somebody somewhere had opened up all the windows in his mind and a cold breeze was blowing through. The sensation was not unpleasant. His first use of this return to sanity was to get his naked feet onto the floor and so escape the clamminess of a mattress saturated by sweat. This he managed to do, though with many premonitions of what life would be like when he was old. He sat with his hands on his knees, his lower lip pushed out, wondering about how to get to the little square window and open it. For the room stank. Open the window, lean out and let the sun warm him. Yes, that was the thing to do. He was still planning how to achieve this when the door opened and Hans Georg walked in, smelling of cows, his boots and gaiters flecked with mud and milk.

'Today you send the telegraph to England,' he

announced.

'Get me some clothes. First, bring me some hot water and a towel. Some coffee and a slice of bread. And something to write with.'

'I see you are better,' the German guffawed. 'I send Anna.'

'No. We will do this my way.'

Hans Georg at least solved the problem of the window, opening it and then posting the sodden mattress through it like a particularly cumbersome parcel.

'Here it stinks. I am not your servant, English. I send Anna. How is your wound?'

'It hurts.'

'Show me, please.'

When Philip fainted, the German carried him downstairs and laid him on a wooden bench in the farm parlour, watched by a very old woman slicing beans.

'Is this the poor man you have robbed so cruelly?' she asked in a rhetorical sort of way. 'He doesn't look much to me.'

He walked outside, found the mattress and threw it on the roof of an outside privy. The first flies arrived, as juicy as blackberries. When he went back inside his grandmother was leaning over the figure on the bench, applying a smouldering chicken feather to Philip's nose.

'Take him outside and put him under the pump,' she suggested. 'The shock will start his heart.'

'I am not dying,' Philip protested. 'A little coffee will set me right.'

'I thought you were English,' the old lady cried.

'He *is* English,' Hans Georg said in great exasperation.

'Then where are his clothes? No Englishman wears only a shirt.'

'Listen, Grandma, you seem a very intelligent woman. I need clothes to be sure but first—' Philip managed a feeble smile—'I need a cup of your coffee and a kind word.'

'Pfft,' she cried uncertainly. 'My last kind word was spoken many years ago. If you wanted coffee you should have come down at five this morning. I am having trouble understanding any of this.'

'I will make him another poultice,' Hans Georg decided.

'Good God,' Grandma exclaimed with great reverence, retreating to her beans. She mumbled to herself for a while and then looked up. 'Some clothes, or at least something to cover his manhood, would be a good idea. But then what do I know? I am just a poor old hunchback with nowhere to go and no one to love me.'

Urgent you bring one hundred sovereigns immediately this address. Of national importance. Sumatra Rules apply, as previously. Come alone. Westland.

Murch studied the telegram form for the fifth or sixth time, smoothing it out with his palm as if to release further meanings from the text. William Kennett's library had come up with some of the goods—the message had originated at a place called Feldhausen which resisted identification but had been passed through another place called Stoppenberg, which did exist as a dot on the map to the east of Essen. The wording was unambiguous and the clue was in the phrase

154

'Sumatra Rules', to be found in a Margam novel called *The Captain's Table*. The phrase spelt blood.

Billy Murch had no idea what Mr Westland was doing in Germany but that hardly came into it and he did not give it another thought. *Where* was not the question. The man was in trouble, maybe deep trouble. Half an hour's silent quizzing of the only evidence—this sorry-looking telegram form addressed to William Munch, MP—was never too long.

His wife Millie came in with a mug of tea strong enough to paint a fence. Murch took her free hand and kissed it.

'Seems he's got himself in a hole,' he said.

'Germany, is it?' Millie asked, peering at the book of maps. 'How far's that, then?'

'A good train ride.'

'And I suppose you'll go?'

'He don't give me much choice. See there? *Of national importance.*'

'What does it mean?'

'Buggered if I know. How much money do we have in the house?'

Millie sat down opposite him and laid a hand on her belly, where the baby pummelled with his tiny fists and danced a gentle hornpipe. Her smile was not without its element of derision.

'You should have been with Robin Hood and all his mates. I suppose you'd go to California if the Kennetts asked you.'

'Stretching it now, girl. No, California a bit out of the way. I don't say as Germany lifts the heart, neither. What would you do, Mill'?'

'Me?' Millie squealed. 'You're asking me?'

Murch waited. He could be as awkward as a sack

155

of ferrets, he knew that, but being married to Millie had tempered his more saturnine aspects. Though he did not always ask her opinion out loud, he had come to depend upon it and could read the weather in her heart as surely as any country bumpkin standing at his garden gate. He loved her. These three words had yet to cross his lips but what else was love, if not this?

'Can you get there in time?' Millie asked.

'You think he's in that sort of danger?'

'Well, he didn't write to the Bishop of Southwark or What's-his-name—'

'The Duke of Cambridge—'

'No. What he wants is cross-eyed Billy Murch to go and hook him out of the mess he's got himself into. The distinguished MP,' she added teasingly.

'You make a good point,' Billy said thoughtfully. 'And all this about a hundred gold sovereigns?'

'Well, he knows you're rich but I'd say he was trying to mark your card along the lines of "nobody will do but you, Billy Boy. It's that urgent, God help me."'

'And what you're saying, we haven't actually got them sovs to hand?' he teased.

'What we've got is a cocoa tin in the kitchen with enough put by to buy the baby his first set of drawers, as well you know.'

'It's a facer,' Murch murmured.

'D'you hear that?' Millie asked her stomach. 'Your father's coming the old soldier with us again.'

'Again?'

Millie reached over and kissed him.

'You were probably born in a ditch with your arse as bare as a cow's bum. This child of yours

156

knows that, already knows that, and he won't take it wrong if you steal the clothes off his back. You've made up your mind to go, you great lummox. I shall want to have words with Mr Westland when you fetch him back, mind.'

'If I can.'

'If you can! I wonder at you sometimes, Murchie, really I do. What, nip over to Germany and find some nothing place that nobody's never heard of? I'd do it myself if it wasn't laundry day.'

'Now you're talking!' Billy said, cracking one of his rare shy smiles.

TWELVE

By the light in the sky, however weak and diffused, Bella judged it to be an hour after daybreak. What before had seemed a grey blank slowly resolved itself into a prospect of distant trees, heavy with water, sleepy with it, so much so that she began to yearn for them with the same hunger she was already experiencing for a plate of egg and bacon, or best of all, a change of clothes. The idea of woodland was somehow comforting, filled with the promise of men with quiet jobs and children gathering mushrooms. Add in friendly dogs and a straggle of geese, why not?

The contours of the land that lay below her had softened, offering broad and largely empty meadows. Bella could make out the pale threads of roads—or at any rate lanes—and the blue smudge of what might be smoke. And all this was tantalisingly close, even as viewed through curtains of rain and the intimidating foreground of bare and scabby moor.

It had been Ursula's characteristically cruel idea to tie a halter round Bella's neck, made from a rotting length of rope found on the floor of the stone hut they sheltered in. The idea was that the free end of the rope would remain wound round her captor's wrist—but of the three women, Ursula was the oldest and, when it came to it, the most incompetent. She lay on her back, snoring noisily, unaware that Bella had slipped the halter without the slightest difficulty and was free to run away any time she liked. What held her back was hunger and—no matter that it was high summer in other parts of the kingdom—bone-chilling cold. When she held her hands out in front of her, she saw that they were lavender blue. Easy enough to explain: there was not a stitch of clothing on her that was not made sodden by rain and mud. Her flesh crawled.

Ursula stirred and gave a tug to the halter, only to find the business end hanging on a rusting nail driven into a roofbeam. She sat up in confusion, peering about her with gummed-up eyes.

'You're not at your best in the mornings, are you?' Bella observed coolly.

'Where is Amelia?'

'She has gone to find us something to eat.'

'Gone, gone where?'

'She didn't mention.'

'Was it she that untied you?'

'You have a very limited sense of story,' Bella snapped. 'You think she untied me and then put me on my honour to stay here and listen to you snoring? And that I said, "very well, Amelia my

158

dear"?'

'Don't take that tone with me. Remember you are still my prisoner.'

'This is breathtaking. The only reason that I do not leave you here alone, you idiotic creature, is that I intend to bring you to justice. Look at me, Lady Ursula! Wake up and look at me! Without that girl, you are helpless. We will wait for Amelia, eat something and hopefully dry our clothes a little. Then we will continue downhill to the world of real things. Unless the police arrive first.'

'You don't understand,' Ursula said with a sudden arresting simplicity. 'I can't be taken.'

'It is too late for all that. Soon, what you are and everything you've done will be known to the world. Everything. Not as rumour and gossip but cold fact.'

'Why are you so filled with hate?'

'I will answer you with another question. What do you know of a woman called Jane Westland?'

Ursula peered at her for a moment. Her slow-breaking smile was horrible to witness. She shook her head in mocking wonderment.

'Well, well,' she muttered. 'That old story. Is that really why you came? There is a brother, I believe. Does he come into it? No doubt he does.'

'Jane Westland,' Bella demanded. Ursula laughed.

'Oh, such a stern voice! Such flashing eyes! You are a meddling fool, Mrs Wallis. You make a very poor avenging fury. Go home to your petty little existence and wring your hands there. Tell your diary what you have seen.'

One wall of the hut was blackened by smoke and in a corner were a few kindling sticks and what was

159

left of a little wicket gate. Bella began searching. Jammed into a hole in the wall was a tin box, the lid depicting the pyramids of Giza. Inside, some provident shepherd had placed some stubs of candle and a handful of varnished matches.

'What are you doing?' Ursula Gollinge yelped.

'I am going to make a fire. To signal the police.'

'Put the box down. Put it down!'

Women do not hit other women. Bella put her hands on Ursula's chest and pushed, enough to send her sprawling. Kicked her in the rump. Found she was shouting. Blood pounded in her ears.

Ursula rolled onto her hands and knees and clawed her way up the wall of the hut.

'Where is Amelia?' she screamed, wide-eyed and dishevelled. Pushing Bella aside she staggered out into the rain.

Running towards her, perhaps a hundred yards away, was an antic figure in a shooting jacket and muddy green corduroys, followed by a boy with red hair. Without a second's hesitation, Ursula turned and ran downhill, tumbling as she went but always bouncing back up. And as Bella watched, she saw a younger, lither figure running diagonally to join her. Then—but all at the same time, like the single shaking of a kaleidoscope—black dots appeared on the moor and the air was pierced by whistles and wild hallooing.

Urmiston crashed into the hut and seized Bella in a trembling embrace.

'Thank God you are safe,' he sobbed, before collapsing and pulling her down on top of him. Bella, laughing and crying, reached out an arm for Alfie and dragged him into the melee.

An orderly withdrawal to Herbert Lintott's lovely house on the road to Grassington was proposed and discounted, likewise the bridal suite at the George. No, nothing would do but Alfie's mother's cottage behind the cattle market and Mrs Stannard's own bed to crawl into. A hot toddy made from whisky and squeezed oranges, with just a dash of honey. Lizzie Stannard's goose-fat embrocation, applied by the lady of the house to Bella's blushing chest. A stone hot-water bottle to the feet. The cat for company.

Downstairs, Urmiston and Alfie sat in a mist of drying clothes, eating something new to the Londoner, fried egg sandwiches. Butter and dribbles of yolk ran down their chins. Tea the thing to drink with fried eggs—huge green mugs of it. Enough sugar to make the teeth ache.

'A couple of choice barmpots you two are,' Mrs Stannard said with great contentment. 'There's any amount of danger out there in the dark. It's a wonder you weren't both sent arse over tip—begging your pardon, Mr Urmiston—into some old mine shaft or such.'

'It was several times on my mind,' Urmiston confessed. 'But your boy is a wonder at the running. Rabbits could hardly do better. And since I was very careful never to let go of his hand, we survived.'

'Well, 'tis the talk of the town. I have had the neighbours coming round to pump my hand since ever you pitched up safe and sound. And how the police do love you for stealing their thunder, I don't think!'

'Have they found the two fugitives?'

'They have not. There's hue and cry all over, trains stopped and searched, all the canal boats with an armed constable on 'em. But not a sign. Not a sausage. My word but that old dressing gown sets you off a treat, Mr Urmiston. Quite the squire, you do look.'

'You spoke of armed constables?'

'Well, perhaps I was exaggerating a touch. But the warrant is out for those two wicked women on a charge of abduction, that I do know.'

'They will want to interview Mrs Wallis, no doubt,' Urmiston reflected uneasily.

'There's no policeman crossing that threshold before I says so,' Lizzie declared, pointing to the front door. 'Or to be more particular about it, before the lady herself says so.'

'Handsomely put, Mrs Stannard.'

'You are kind to say so. Now Alfie, do you take the gentleman upstairs—but quietly now—and go through the chest of your father's things and kit him out with some suitable duds. Paying attention,' she added meaningfully, 'to the fact that your dadda had but the one good suit and otherwise a taste for fabric that would shame a circus.'

'Is your father dead?' Urmiston whispered as they tiptoed upstairs.

'No. In Ireland, where he came from. Went out to buy some meat for our supper one night and never came back.'

'How long ago was this?'

'Ancient times. We don't miss him,' Alfie added.

'But, erm, was he a big man? Say about my size, would you say?'

'He was a giant,' the boy said, stifling a laugh

162

and vaguely remembering just that—a red-headed giant with a taste for the stout and the knack of bending pokers in half.

*   *   *

The police called in the late afternoon. Inspector Bullard was a grave and methodical fellow in his fifties with something of the soldier about him. Bella wondered what that might be and found the answer in his unblinking calm. It was as though the inspector had spent an adult lifetime watching wickedness pass in parade, so much so that he had lost the capacity to be surprised.

The facts of the case were soon established. Bella had been lifted, as Bullard put it, by Amelia Jackson and carried to the house of Lady Ursula Gollinge. There she had been imprisoned for five days and nights in what she took to be a storage cellar, only being brought out to listen to what she called ranting monologues. Bullard was uncomfortable with the adjective—too wayward, too fanciful.

'Can you say a little more about the nature of this ranting?'

'That only simple people have any idea of the shape of the world and the only simple people left are what we in our ignorance call savages.'

'Savages?'

'I can't help you, Inspector,' Bella smiled. 'But Lady Gollinge has a very low view of civilisation. Things went to pot when the world gave up hunter-gathering, you understand. We grew fat and incredibly lazy. Our souls grew ugly. We turned to torture and exploitation as a way of life.'

163

'My word,' Bullard exclaimed, without losing a jot of his general imperturbability.

'Of course,' Bella continued, 'in those happier times any self-respecting hunter-gatherer would have knocked her on the head without a qualm of conscience. If indeed conscience ever came into it.'

'Weren't they morally superior to us?'

'Whether they were or not, Lady Gollinge would have been a strong candidate for being left behind or bashed on the head. I think for her, the idea of searching for nuts and berries is not work, but pleasure. Rather like picking daisies, or picnicking in the bluebell woods.'

'I am sorry to have missed it,' the inspector said sourly. 'Was anything else spoken of in these rants?'

'I'm afraid men came in for it hot and strong,' Bella smiled. 'White men, that is. The English in particular.'

'Yes,' Bullard nodded gloomily. 'A poor set of folk, white men. Now, Mrs Wallis, I will ask you this: Did either woman mention the name Raybould in the course of these rants? Or at any other time?'

'I know who Raybould is, of course,' she havered.

'From the hermit, yes. You had his character from Duxbury. But did his name come up when you were with the women? A white man, to be sure. And as English as Mr Gladstone. What you might call a neighbour of theirs out on the moors. A fellow who shared their happy hunting grounds, so to speak. Shared them—or ruined them. Do you follow my drift, Mrs Wallis?'

'I do indeed, Inspector Bullard.'

'And so how do you answer? I will put it plainly to you,' Bullard added. 'If enough evidence can be brought forward, then we shall be contemplating a charge of murder.'

'She killed Raybould?' Bella asked, alarmed.

'That is what I am trying to find out. Raybould was murdered, you can be sure of that.'

One part of Bella wanted to see Ursula become the victim of a sensational criminal trial and suffer all the consequences. Let the white men she despised so much take their revenge on her and make her name a subject of contempt all over Britain. The temptation for Bella to perjure herself was very strong. But honesty held her back—that and an unexpected pity for the confused and farcical woman. Bullard was all this time watching her carefully. It was as though, without either of them moving, he had manoeuvred her into the darkest corner of the room. Bella felt beads of perspiration on her upper lip.

'I do not remember them mentioning his name.'

The inspector sat back, his face still inscrutable, the movement alone betraying his dissatisfaction. Bella flushed.

'Certainly they claimed they knew how to deal with importunate men and there was a lot of giggling at that,' she suggested.

'Did they name anyone?'

'I have told you, no.'

'And what is importunate when it's at home?'

'Most women would understand me.'

'Do you say so?' Bullard growled.

'The only time I had seen Lady Gollinge before my capture was in conversation with the girl

165

Amelia at the George Hotel. She spoke very freely and illiberally then and I took her to mean that sort of thing in general. Men, I mean.'

Bullard fell to plucking at his ear lobe, still with his eyes fixed on hers.

'Mr Urmiston has told me how you retrieved Raybould's remains,' she offered.

'Mmm.'

'And that the injury to the skull could hardly have been accidental.'

'Ah! Is Mr Urmiston a surgeon then? A bit of an expert, is he? We have him down as a shopkeeper.'

'Mr Bullard, I cannot tell you what I did not hear. You want me to say that I heard them confess to killing poor Mr Raybould. I did not.'

'Lady Gollinge threatened to kill you, though?'

'More than once.'

'And why was that?'

Bella did not have a ready answer. All at once, Bullard seemed to indicate that the interview was coming to an end, for he began fussing grumpily with a pipe and its pouch. She felt the most ridiculous guilt at not giving him the answer he wanted.

'Why should she want to kill you?' he repeated.

'Do you know, Inspector, I have no idea.'

'Unless, of course, it was in her nature.' He raised his pale blue eyes from the business of teasing out his tobacco. 'Or that she'd done it before. And was not sure how much the hermit had told you. Or was threatened by you coming up from London, for reasons we have yet to hear.'

'Is that how it looks?' Bella asked faintly.

'Any way you look at it, a lady from London turns up and is very far from being welcomed.

Quite the contrary, in fact.'

'Inspector, I ask you to believe that until I came to Yorkshire I had never met Lady Gollinge in my life. She has a certain reputation in some circles as a deeply disturbed individual. That was all I knew of her.'

'And so, why did you come?'

Bella hesitated. Since her final confrontation with Ursula Gollinge she had found time to think. Dragging Jane Westland's name into the inquiry could do nothing but harm to Philip and might threaten her relationship to the man she loved most in the world. How to explain to this stolid Yorkshire policeman her arrogance—and wasn't that the word for it?—in believing she could shame a madwoman into repentance? Bullard watched these emotions flit across her face with a dreadful calm of his own.

'You were going to tell me why you came up north to meet her,' he said.

'I was curious,' Bella mumbled. The lameness of the remark was enough to make her blush.

The inspector pinched the bridge of his nose as if the pain of what she had just said had landed there, like the beginnings of a headache. In Mrs Stannard's sitting room the time was told by a German alarm clock that was carried down from the bedroom each morning. Its metallic clack was the only sound in the room for more than a minute.

'As far as I know there is no law against that,' Bella said.

Bullard thought about lighting his pipe and then regretfully put it away in his pocket. He smoothed crumbs of tobacco from his lap. She was being dismissed.

'You've had a bit of a do with the lady, and you've come out of it largely unharmed. Be thankful, as I'm sure you are. You'll no doubt be wanting to get back to London as soon as possible.'

'I hadn't begun to think of it.'

'Mr Urmiston has already booked your tickets, I believe.'

'Has he, indeed? He had no right to do that.'

'Perhaps it is the London way. There's importunate and importunate,' Inspector Bullard muttered.

*   *   *

London was the antidote to these adventures, there was no doubt about that.

'It is being home among your own things,' Mrs Venn explained Bella's mood, as if to a child. 'Sleeping in your own bed again. There is no better medicine. You have been among a very sorry lot and it's a miracle to me how you got by. Did you take a meal with this Mrs Stannard, by any chance?'

'You mustn't be jealous of her, Dora. You two would get along famously.'

'I doubt it,' Dora Venn declared. 'You have come home not much bigger than a skinned rabbit, Mrs Wallis, and your face as drawn as Mr Merriboy's, the chimney sweep, before they fixed his waterworks. And the clothes you set out in not fit to wear again. Now, I hope we shall have no argument about this but I have in mind a steak-and-kidney pie and a plate of the newest of new potatoes.'

168

'Dora, I would eat a raw herring if you put one before me.'

She took a bath and washed her hair, dressed herself in a high-necked linen blouse and wool skirt, meaning to go downstairs and glide about from room to room while waiting for her meal. But when Dora Venn came to look for her, she found her mistress curled up like a child and fast asleep. Leaning over Bella to wake her, she was astonished to have her start up with every appearance of terror. And then the tears began, blabbing tears. The two women sat side by side on the edge of the bed, their arms round each other, howling. Dora knew that small though the Orange Street house was, without Philip Westland in it Bella had found it as echoing and empty as the Albert Hall.

'Hush, hush,' she murmured groggily, her throat full of her own sobs. 'They can hear us out in the street, I am sure, and will think the cat has died.'

'Dora, let us eat together tonight, not downstairs in the kitchen but in the dining room.'

'Good Lord above,' Mrs Venn exclaimed. 'That would never do! I shall sit by you and watch you tuck away my pie, in more of a nursie way, if you like. But sit down with you to eat? I never heard of such a wicked idea in all my years. I should never be able to look Mrs Bardsoe in the eye again. We'll sail this ship on an even keel.'

'Then where is he, Mrs Venn? Why wasn't he here to greet me?' Bella wailed. Dora kissed her cheek.

'Mr Philip? Looking for his socks, I don't wonder, and fussing over his blessed train timetables. There's only so much abroad a man

169

can take, in my opinion. I believe he got as far as Cairo once and then doubled back for the love of you.'

'I have never told you that story.'

'No, but he did,' Dora Venn lied cheerfully. In fact, she had the bones of it from that wicked old scoundrel Percy Quigley, whose whole purpose in life was to mind other people's business. She pulled Bella up.

'I shall expect you downstairs in ten minutes,' she smiled shakily. 'As for that old Lady Gollinge, if she ain't taken up by the police already, she's hiding in a ditch somewhere. So we can put her out of our mind. And good riddance!'

*   *   *

Ursula Gollinge was neither in custody nor cowering in a ditch. She was sitting in a gardener's hut in Roundhay Park, Leeds, having earlier robbed the Vicar of Roundhay of his parish funds, a change of clothes and some other knick-knacks that were too tempting to pass up. (The Reverend Mr Loveridge was at the Town Hall with his wife and daughters, listening to a concert of sacred music and finding it excessively boring. His true purpose in being there was to be in the same space, however huge, as one of his parishioners, a Mrs Neal. When he came home later that evening and found his house burgled, it seemed to him like divine punishment. His wife, who knew all about Mrs Neal, considered it the price one paid for leaving open a ground-floor window.)

The park-keeper's hut was Amelia's idea and smelled agreeably of mown grass and engine oil.

When it was fully dark, the two women planned to walk down into Leeds and see how the trains ran. But for the time being they shared cold cuts from a sirloin of beef taken from the vicarage kitchen.

'I have never been to London,' Amelia said with a tinge of doubt in her voice.

'You will love it. And I will change, you'll see.'

'How will we live? For money, I mean.'

'I don't in the least mind robbing another house or two.'

Amelia watched her lover masticate. It was not a pleasant sight and the sound was disgusting. The plain fact was that the further Ursula Gollinge was from the moors around Cruddas the less lovable she was. The girl made allowance for the fact that the wild-haired hunter-gatherer was wearing Mrs Loveridge's garden-party best, the seams of which were already split under the arms to accommodate a far more generous bust than the vicar's wife could offer the world. But what had seemed blithe in Skipton seemed merely stupid now.

'And what if we come across Mrs Wallis?' she asked.

'Oh, I know how to destroy her,' Ursula replied cheerfully. 'She is the least of our worries. No, we shall have new names and, I fancy, a little cottage in somewhere like Chelsea.'

'And we'll set up as burglars, shall we?'

'To begin with.'

'You don't think we'd be safer a bit further from London?'

'As soon as we have the fares, we shall take ship for Australia. I have told you this, child, a thousand times. I cannot reward your loyalty more highly.'

It was agreed that while Ursula might take a cab

to the station, if one could be found, it was folly for them to be seen together. Accordingly, Amelia must walk, or—if she thought it safe—take a tram.

She elected to walk. Ursula never saw her again.

THIRTEEN

Next day, it was Bella's whim to go to lunch at her favourite restaurant, Fracatelli's. As a way of cheering herself up, nothing could be better chosen, for this was a place she associated with all the good things in her life, a little haven of elegance set down in the otherwise brutally unromantic Strand. The restaurant, with its famous chandeliers, was neighboured on one side by a narrow house converted to half a dozen one-room offices. On the other was a theatrical costumier's that had seen better days. Sandwiched between, and with the same unimposing facade, Fracatelli had created a shrine to Mediterranean high seriousness without any of the self-advertisement that went with bigger premises in more favoured locations. His clientele were the very willing guardians of a well-kept secret.

Fracatelli never refused a customer but made sure that the worst of them never returned. American tourists who tried to talk down the bill and members of the House of Lords whose manners left something to be desired found on their next visit that, alas, all tables were reserved for the evening. The French got short shrift; especially, for some dark reason, those from Mentone. Children were tolerated for Sunday lunch only. Bella was the only unaccompanied woman ever to dine there. Her current bête noire, Cissie Cornford, considered Fracatelli the rudest man in London, an eminence he shared with the bleak old Duke of Cambridge, to whom she had once spoken eight unanswered words at an Aldershot Review.

'The fellow seems to forget he is Italian,' the painter Frith complained to Bella, after being refused a table for the simple faux pas of turning up in a peasant straw hat.

'It is because he *never* forgets he is Italian that the food is so good,' she retorted.

She dressed for this particular lunch in a favourite sprigged muslin gown that by its chic more or less commanded the rain to stop. And so it did, leaving the pavements smelling of wet pennies, lit by a sun smiling on London from somewhere over Green Park. This change in the weather did much to improve the capital's temper, so that perfect strangers exchanged nods and becks and even the cabbies were good-natured. The air was filled with the jingle of harness and hearty greetings from flower sellers and anyone else with wares to hawk. Balloon men were doing a brisk trade. Toy soldiers mustered and marched in Long Acre. Outside the Royal Opera House, a man was eating fire. Quigley had a cherished phrase for all this impromptu—the dear old city was showing her drawers.

Signor Fracatelli had caught the changing mood. He fussed over Bella, snapping his fingers to summon Alberto, one of the younger waiters. They discussed what La Signora might eat; meanwhile, a deliciously crisp spumante was proposed and

173

accepted. Fracatelli himself uncorked the bottle, the better to complete the story of his niece's wedding to (imagine it!) a Danish boy from Esbjerg with already six ships in his fleet. Maybe not so big, these vessels; in fact, not much more than herring boats. But a young man with good manners and not a scrap of self-doubt in his make-up.

'And where did they take their honeymoon?' Bella asked. Fracatelli put his thumb to his cheek and flicked.

'St Petersburg! Can anyone explain this? She is surely the first Italian girl to go there, I mean from choice. My sister—her mother—cried for a week when she was told. But I do not need to tell you, signora. Love is blind, a most fortunate thing for Danes with blonde moustaches.'

'Is not your niece very beautiful?'

Fracatelli shrugged and gave the pristine tablecloth a last pass with his napkin. He dumped the wine bottle in its bucket of ice and span it with his fingers, producing a noise that always gave Bella a tiny frisson of her own.

'Like I'm telling you, love is blind,' he sighed. 'Which explains why all marriages are happy at the beginning. To answer your question, she is a little on the heavy side.'

Bella chose a dish of chicken livers and black grapes in a Madeira sauce, followed by a very welcome salad. The young Alberto hovered, his eyes as softly lashed as a girl's. She was on her second tiny cup of coffee when a shadow fell across the table.

'Mrs Wallis,' Sir Edward Havelock murmured. 'I was just on my way when I recognised you and

174

thought to pay my respects.'

Havelock had more of the courtier about him than senior policeman. He was very tall and (though he was sixty) decidedly boyish in appearance. His white hair flopped forward over his brow and he had retained since youth that manner of tucking his chin into his chest, as if apologising for his existence to anyone not of his own class. A gentle smile peeked out from a lined and weary face.

'Will you not sit down, Sir Edward? I am poised between ordering a grappa and not. I should be very happy if you would help me make up my mind.'

The Assistant Commissioner had a much-remarked social knack. It was said of him by awed hostesses that he was either in the room or not, never to be seen entering, never taking his leave. This gift extended to sitting down. One moment he was towering over Bella and the next completely at his ease in the free chair at her table. He might as well have been there for the last hour.

'You have had some adventures in Yorkshire recently,' he said without preamble, as though changing the subject from the care of heated greenhouses, where to buy reliable oysters, or anything else they might have been talking about.

'Have they arrested her?' Bella asked eagerly.

'I fear not. There has been a great deal of breast-beating and the crying of woe about this in Yorkshire but I don't find it untoward.' He hesitated. 'The girl—'

'Amelia—'

'Yes, was found in Hull. Unfortunately, with her throat cut.'

175

Bella felt her eyes well. When she looked down at her hands, she saw they trembled.

'Poor creature!' she managed to say.

'It does seem a shame,' Havelock agreed politely.

'How did this happen? Do we know?'

'She was unlucky enough to fall foul of a Russian deckhand without a word of English. This man was in turn murdered by those who witnessed the killing, which took place in a notorious dockside drinking den. It was all very sudden and very violent. Perhaps she deserved better.'

'Certainly she did. She was an intelligent girl. I liked her.'

Sir Edward tapped the table with his signet ring and bestowed on Bella his most affectionate smile.

'I believe only you among your sex could say such a thing, after having been so cruelly abducted, Mrs Wallis.'

'Believe me, I think much less well of her partner. Was Lady Gollinge with her when she died?'

'The people they have up there think not; nor does it seem very likely. If I had to guess I'd say she was making her way to London, if not already here.'

'And is this why you stopped by my table, Sir Edward?'

Havelock pursed his lips, before giving Bella his shrewdest glance.

'I thought you would want to know we are alert to the situation. A description has been issued to all divisions, yes. And you are of concern to me, rather more than I could wish.'

'As, for example?'

'Reflect a moment. Lady Gollinge has no idea what you might or might not have said to the police in Skipton that will make matters worse for her. It is just possible she may wish to renew acquaintance.'

'But here, of course, I am on my own ground.'

'Yes,' Havelock murmured.

'I don't claim to know London well but there are certain parts of it known to me of which Lady Gollinge is, and will always remain, utterly ignorant. She fights on such ground at her peril.'

And never say more to a policeman than is absolutely necessary, she added instantly, greatly angered at herself. She searched for the phrase she wanted and grimaced when she found it: never prate.

'I know you to be a courageous and doughty fighter,' Sir Edward agreed.

Something in the way he spoke set off warning bells as loud as any fire engine. Bella studied the backs of her hands. Havelock seemed to find some detail at the far end of the room interesting.

'Are we talking about my ability to take care of myself?' she asked at length. 'Is it unfeminine for a woman to defend herself with all the means at her disposal?'

'My dear Mrs Wallis,' the Assistant Commissioner protested, laughing. He swept a crumb of bread away with the back of his hand and wiggled a forefinger in his ear with comical energy. Bella waited. The ear-wiggling was a punctuation mark. She guessed what was coming next.

'I believe you have been pestered recently by an officer of mine. You'll forgive me if I choose not to name him.'

'Was I being pestered?' Bella countered swiftly, as if watching a bomb roll towards her, its fuse spluttering. Havelock spent some more moments glancing round the restaurant in an abstracted way before returning his mild gaze to hers.

'He was perhaps being merely overzealous. It happens to some young detectives. However it was, four nights ago the uniformed police were called to help the unfortunate fellow down from a signal gantry at King's Cross. He was hanging by his ankles, covered head to foot in whitewash.'

Murch! thought Bella exultantly.

'How extraordinary,' she said, managing to keep her expression girlishly attentive. 'Had he fallen foul of some criminal gang?'

'He remembers being hit on the head from behind and so forth, but very little else. He is—or was—attached to the Snow Hill station. I'm afraid he made himself very unpopular with the natives in that part of the world. That might be one explanation of events.'

Or not, Sir Edward Havelock's steady gaze suggested.

'Might I ask what any of this has to do with me, Sir Edward?' Bella asked, determined to call him out. 'I think I was in Yorkshire at the time.'

'Indeed you were. But let us put it this way, Mrs Wallis. You are lucky to have the friendship and loyalty of some very admirable people. We might say they patrol your best interests. And long may they continue to do so. But—' he added, tapping out these last words with his fingers on Fracatelli's snowy tablecloth—'there will be no more high jinks.'

'You choose a strange expression, Sir Edward.'

178

'Yes,' Havelock murmured. 'It is odd, to be sure. Let me speak even more plainly. At the first sight of Lady Gollinge in London—at the merest hint of her presence here—you will report yourself to the nearest police station. Dear me, dear me,' he added, with a mirthless chuckle. 'What a roundabout way of telling you to be careful. But I think you take my point. On all counts.'

He rose and extended his hand. Then, in that mysterious way of his, he was gone.

*　　　*　　　*

'And didn't I tell you not to go up to them heathen parts alone?' Captain Quigley scolded. He himself was back from Portsmouth with adventures of his own to relate—a close run-in with an over-amorous landlady and some complications with certain crates and cartons stamped 'VR'.

'I was out of my depth,' Quigley confessed. 'They do things differently down there. Not that every second cove you meet isn't bent as a butcher's hook. But the scale is different. At one stage I was stuck holding two hundred solar topees marked for Chandrapur. Don't ask me how.'

'I have no intention of doing anything of the kind,' Bella said. 'If you remember, the conversation we are supposed to be having is about Sergeant Tubney.'

'Yes, and how did *that* happen?' Quigley countered. 'He must have enemies we know nothing of. The whitewash a particularly bold stroke. And you may not have heard but Topper Lawson has been in the wars likewise. Found nailed to a hoarding by his overcoat, his boots on

179

the wrong feet and a dunce's hat on his head. Well, it don't surprise me. He had it coming. Between them they had it coming.'

'Where is Billy Murch?' Bella demanded abruptly.

'Billy? Now what's he got to do with it?'

'Never mind that! Where is he?'

'Am I my brother's keeper? I did call over to Chiswick a couple of nights ago for a wet and a bit of a gab and Millie reports he's gone down to Chatham. Did you have something you wanted to ask him, dear lady?'

'An hour ago, I was warned off any further nonsense by Sir Edward Havelock. In the nicest possible way but—and understand me, Captain—definitively.'

'Good Lord!' Quigley exclaimed. 'Definitive, was it? That must have brought you up short in your tracks. Sir Edward known to be a flaming firebrand of an individual, the hammer and coking tongs of the fight against crime. My word, who would want to come up against *him* down a dark alley?'

'One day your facetiousness will get the better of you,' Bella fumed.

Quigley had an answer to that, too. He indicated the battered rosewood table, on which lay a neat stack of paper, her pen and a bottle of black ink. True, there was also a plate of empty whelk shells that he disposed of by chucking the contents through the open door; but the point stood.

'Looking after you, Mr Margam, sir, can be brisk work. For as long as you sit at that table, you will need the help and comfort of lesser mortals such as myself. We have seen very recent how you

180

are when you're on your own. Next to useless, if you'll pardon the expression.'

'I am thinking of closing the office down.'

'Moving your base of operations temporarily. Agreed!'

'Shutting it down. Nailing up the front door. Quitting.'

Quigley goggled. What was Margam's office was also his quarters, his place of abode. It was, if a person wanted to put it this way, his support trench, firestep and sally port.

'Now we don't want to be doing nothing hasty,' he said. 'The dear old Court has been a friend to us both. And I fancy there have been some rare strokes of literature composed at that table there. I mind how before Captain Deveril met his disgrace he hovered for more than a week poised between love and dishonour before being given a hearty shove by your good self when you was in a better mood and fortified by the Captain's Dutch gin in the stone bottle.'

'Which I never wish to taste again.'

'A delicacy greatly sought after by the more discerning palate.'

'Quigley, arguing with you is like trying to sculpt in frogspawn.'

'Yes,' he flashed back. 'And how did you first come by that useful phrase? From Welsh Phil is how, here in this very place. Abandon the Court? The Bard of Avon would have been pleased to get his feet under that table. Welsh Phil, College Pete, Billy Murch himself, not to mention Charlie Urmiston in all his pomp—'

'Suppose I say the game is up?'

'Then, dear lady, Mr Margam, sir, you would be

181

making a sorry error of judgement. An egregious mistake,' he added, without the slightest idea of what the last adjective meant.

But Bella was wholly serious. She had come so close to saying too much to Ursula Gollinge and fighting Philip Westland's battles for him. It was as though loving him as much as she did gave her the licence to touch on the one secret torment he would never allow to be discussed. Shutting up the Fleur de Lys office was a guilty gesture, therefore, an act of contrition. The truth was that no amount of book-writing could ever replace love in the real world. With a sudden jump in her heart, she realised she might never take up a pen again.

Quigley watched her with one of his rare fits of perspicacity. It was as if he knew exactly what she was thinking and she could read in his eyes a certain shy but sincere kindliness, even. She jutted out her chin and faced him down.

'You don't understand,' she improvised. 'I have to defend myself against this Gollinge woman.'

'Ho! If she has come to London. And if she has, how would she ever know how to find you?'

'She has the Orange Street address.'

The Captain looked at Bella with a strange fondness, as sometimes happens when children say something so ineffably stupid that adult reality shivers like a dish of jelly that has been jogged. All this while, he had been wearing his park-keeper's kepi, headgear that he liked so much for its quasi-military associations. Sighing, he took it off and stood there like Livingstone staring numbly at Stanley.

'Never a dull moment in your employ,' he managed to croak.

Billy Murch was not in Chatham, of course, but marching up a muddy lane that led through the railway yards in Essen. Asking after this place Stoppenberg, as mentioned in Philip's telegram, he had fallen in with a far too obliging cove who claimed it was but a cock's stride away. No, no, my friend, really just over there, look, a few hundred metres only! But as the railway tracks ended and a few shabby-looking cottages came into sight, this Samaritan began to act up. He stopped his cheery grunting and babbling and became more thoughtful than was strictly necessary. A cudgel appeared in his hand. When he looked round, Billy had disappeared behind a linesman's hut. The guide walked back to investigate and was caught a blow across the side of his head with a muddy pick helm.

'*Kamerad!*' he yelped, staggering. Murch helped him upright by a hand round his throat.

'See, like you was telling me, you are fond of the old Englanders and I thank you for that. But I wasn't born yesterday. Do I look as if I was born yesterday?'

He pointed to the row of grimy cottages.

'Is that Stoppenberg?'

'No,' the man admitted, blood from his temple pouring into his eyes.

'Is there a pub there? Pub? Boozer?'

'*Stube, ja.*'

'Well then, let's have no more arsing about, no bad feelings, and we'll step across there and share a glass.'

But the man who had wanted to rob him turned on his heel and legged it, his overcoat streaming out behind him. Murch watched him hurdle a small stack of railway sleepers and disappear round the corner of a substantial brick building, one in which every single window had been broken. An engine shed, Billy guessed. Or maybe some kind of workshop. But never Stoppenberg, not for a single bloody minute. He threw down the pick helm and began walking. As it happened, he was going in the right direction, which was to say east.

To an outside observer, there was nothing nervous or guilty about Murch, nor was there the slightest concession to the novelty of his surroundings. When he came to the row of cottages, he found washing lines strung across the road, bearing sheets and nondescript items, fresh from the copper but already flecked with smuts. To make his way, he had to push these aside, so that he had the fancy of walking downstage, over and over. One or two pipe-smoking women watched him pass without comment—a foreigner to be sure, but not one to mess with lightly. A dog a very good indicator of what was what—several dogs sat up at his passing but not one came to challenge.

The truth was, Billy was carrying within him an entirely novel sensation. How this came about—a trick of the light, the soapy smell of the laundered sheets, the otherwise eerie emptiness of the streets, a touch of indigestion even—he could not say; but he wished Millie was with him. She was in any case right there in the forefront of his mind. It was a colossal surprise. Dear old Millie with her raucous laugh, her unapologetic way of breaking wind, the dab hand she gave to apple pie, her

184

conversations with the unborn baby. What a time to think of her! It was enough to make a cove blush. Him, as had so accustomed himself to the solitary life that his entire reputation came to depend upon it!

'You never know what the beggar is thinking,' Quigley was fond of saying, not without awe in his voice. It was a habit that long preceded the Quigley years. Private Murch, as he then was, had distinguished himself as a soldier in the Crimea for just this capacity to keep himself to himself.

'I am done for,' the wounded Major Cathcart had wept. 'You may as well put me down, you dog, for your confounded jogging is shaking the lifeblood out of me.'

As Cathcart told the story later (and it was difficult to head him off from it, as his long-suffering wife knew only too well) this taciturn soldier had run the major two miles over broken ground to the head of the road into Balaclava.

'Slung over his back like a sack of potatoes. I make no bones about it, I was crying like a damned parlourmaid: but from him not a single word. He did not utter. Russian shells bursting all about, the ground littered with dead horses. Amazing fellow. The surgeons told me afterwards they wanted to examine him for wounds, so much blood was there on his tunic. It was all *my* blood, by God! And do you know—' the major always concluded, for he had very little sense of story—'I never clapped eyes on him again! To the extent that the parson here once suggested I had dreamed him. Dreamed the whole bang-shoot. That he had never existed and it was the hand of God that saved me! Rum, what?'

Murch's version of the same events: had come

across this tubby officer crawling about on his hands and knees, whimpering like a dog. Decided to save the cove's life. Spur of the moment thing. Ground a bit tricky but downhill all the way. He told the story while it was fresh in his mind, eating horsemeat steaks with a couple of chancers who had the word 'deserters' written all over them. Well, to say he told the story was an exaggeration: he had it dragged out of him by his incredulous audience. Paid for his steak with a pinch of tobacco and walked away, back to the lines.

But now! Billy, you have changed, he told himself wryly, feeling as light and blown as thistledown. Walking east to Stoppenberg with Millie for company—this is a turn-up for the book and no error. There is something in your heart that was never there before, that disqualifies you from biffing your way to eternity. Fetch Mr Westland out from whatever scrape he's got himself into and go home to your wife and child. And if there's a bit of an opportunity on the road back, give old Westland a nudge in the same direction. Show him the light, as Millie would put it. Lead him into the paths of righteousness. He'll thank you for it, blind me if he won't.

It was an incredibly liberating moment. Watery sunshine drenched the fields on either side, showing off hectares of slumbering cabbages—and in the distance, an embanked road along which plodded three carts and a file of peasanty-looking characters, every man jack of them singing. And here was an instant dividend from having Millie in your head—though Murch was about as musical as a wheelbarrow, he knew from churchgoing with his wife of a Sunday that what he was hearing was a hymn. One of the good old ones, in fact.

FOURTEEN

Philip Westland knew very little of the workings of his own body—in that respect he was one of the shyest men Bella had ever met, a reticence that shaded, when sickness came in one form or another, into downright cowardice. There never was a good time to discuss illness with him. Anything below the waist was completely beyond his powers to mention, as for example when he had poisoned himself with a bit of bad fish and spent three days flitting between the water closet and the spare room, doubled over in agony but too ashamed to ask for help. (On this particular occasion, his life was saved by Hannah Bardsoe, bustling into the house in Orange Street with a cure-all pill the size of a hen's egg: this and the hysterical laughter he could hear as Bella and Mrs Bardsoe discussed his case did the trick. It was a case of governing his wayward guts or dying of indignation.)

The wound to his shoulder was out of a different box. The fever dreams were gone, leaving in their place a clear mind savaged by a barking headache and—at the site of the wound itself—an ugly darkening of the flesh. Some of this was bruising but the suppuration that leaked from the blackened bullet hole itself was too frightening to contemplate. Philip began to believe the flesh was mortifying. When the heat in his shoulder began to spread across his chest, he was forced to confess as much to his captor, Hans Georg. After a bad-tempered examination—and an alarming amount of tooth-sucking—the farmer prepared a salve that resembled (and perhaps was) cooked spinach. When he applied it at near boiling point, straight from the stove, the patient fainted clean away.

'In the name of God!' Hans Georg's old mother exclaimed. 'He is not a beast. What you shove up a cow's arse might not work on an Englishman.'

When Philip came to, he was outside, flat on his back behind a low stone wall. His bloodied shirt lay over him. He was holding someone's hand—he guessed from its weight and softness, Anna's. He squeezed; and after a second or two, was squeezed back. Hans Georg passed him a hand-rolled cigarette.

'It wasn't me who shot you,' he grumbled.

'I am grateful to you for what you have done.'

'Yes, well, your friends from England had better arrive soon,' the German muttered. 'For if you don't get to a doctor, you will die.'

'Then get me to a doctor.'

To which there was no reply, for Philip knew that once lodged with a qualified doctor, his captors would lose control over him; and with that, any chance of the hundred sovereigns they supposed Murch was bringing.

'If I die,' he said, 'the retribution that will fall on you then will be terrible indeed.'

'You seem to forget you are a foreign spy.'

'So? Why not put on a clean shirt and go to see Herr Krupp and tell him the man he is looking for has been hidden from him for nearly a week by two bumpkins trying to extract a reward from the British Foreign Office? What's the matter, don't

188

you have the stomach for that?'

'There had better be a reward,' Hans Georg threatened. 'Because I am getting sick of the sight of you, Englander.'

After he had gone, Philip dragged himself upright with Anna's help.

'If your friend doesn't come, my father will kill you,' she whispered. 'And if not him, then certainly his sister and her husband.'

'The postman and his wife.'

'Yes,' Anna said mournfully. 'We are not very intelligent people, I think.'

'Listen, Anna. The man who is coming is not a weakling like me. He has not come to negotiate. Do you understand?'

'There are no sovereigns?' she asked, a hand to her mouth.

'No. Instead there is a man who is utterly ruthless—believe me—whose sole purpose is to get me out of here, no matter what it takes.'

'My father has a shotgun,' the girl said, her lip trembling.

'A gun won't save him. If he is fool enough to discharge it, or even point it, he is a dead man. But you can help.'

'Me?' she squeaked.

'We shall need a pony and trap. If not that, a horse. A means of escape. If we get away, you have my word no harm will come to you.'

'A horse! There are only five horses in the whole village!'

'What about the pastor? How does he get about?'

'You want me to steal the pastor's horse?' she cried incredulously.

The old lady, who had been listening to all this with grim enjoyment, suddenly scrambled to her feet.

'Run and fetch the bed sheets,' she commanded. 'Two strangers are coming into the yard. Be quick, child.'

To make sure Philip did not show himself above the wall, she put a bare and blackened foot against his throat.

'My son will hold them off for a moment. But we are duty bound to offer them hospitality. Anna will cover you with the sheets. Lie still. And don't breathe.'

'Let me crawl somewhere now.'

'Do as I say. I'll tell you when to crawl.'

Anna reappeared with her arms filled with sheets. When they were dumped over him, Philip stifled a disgusted sob. But Grandma had found an actress within herself. He heard a stinging slap.

'Yes, and didn't I ask you to do this first thing? And now we've got visitors, to our great shame! Don't just stand there. Go and light the boiler.'

*   *   *

Murch had already come across the two strangers, bad-tempered men in town suits and starched collars. Murch in a ditch of watercress, the two men sitting with their legs dangling over the tailboard of a bullock cart as it passed in a cloud of mud. They were cursing, as well they might. Although Murch had not a word of German, he could piece their story together easily enough— tired of walking, they had hitched a ride they now regretted. Both a little bit drunk, one short and fat, the other a more formidable proposition, a lean-looking cove in a soft black hat. A detail: the thin one sat with his fists on his knees—big hands, knobby knuckles. Drunk, but dangerous.

When it was safe to come out of the ditch, Murch sat with his back to a tree, letting the water drain from his clothes, and thinking. These two might be harmless chancers who had wandered in from some other story but he did not believe it. Billy had walked clean through Stoppenberg an hour earlier with a hunter's instinct that he had yet to come upon the freshest trail. There was just enough of what he considered civilisation in the main street for him to discount it as Mr Westland's hidey-hole. There happened to be half a dozen packmen selling ribbons and bonnets outside the village inn and the faces of the women gathered around were far too frank and open. Stoppenberg, as far as these things go, was an innocently happy place. He was even accompanied for a hundred yards or so by a child who held his hand and skipped along beside him, chattering merrily.

The lane he was on now had more promise, if only in the sense that the country round about was more woebegone. The cabbage fields had given way to thickets of blackthorn and the occasional ancient and untenanted cottage. Super sensitive to atmosphere, Billy considered the road to Feldhausen far more likely to lead to something dark and sinister. Sighting the two strangers in the cart had done nothing to diminish this idea: What were obvious townies doing clattering through Mr No-man's-land in their Sunday best? Not police, he judged. But not Bible salesmen either.

The short fat man did the talking. Of the two of them, he was the more obviously drunk. His companion sat in Hans Georg's kitchen smoking and drumming his fingers. He looked bored and under-employed.

'My name is Wrangl,' the fat one blustered. 'It isn't my idea of a day out to come to this shit-heap. So let's get it over with. We are looking for an Englishman. When we find him, we will take him back to Essen. For the people among whom we find him, that's the end of the story. Nothing bad happens to them.'

'Is there an Englishman here? In Feldhausen? How can that be?' the old lady cried in a wondering sort of voice. 'Don't they have cabbages and potatoes in England? It seems a long way to come. But maybe he is mad. Old Sturmer went off his chump and they came for him.'

'Sturmer?'

'A neighbour,' Hans Georg supplied.

'When was this?'

'When she was still a girl.'

Wrangl ran his tongue over his teeth, thought about saying something, changed his mind.

'Naturally, I have never seen an Englishman but then I've never seen a Chinaman, either,' the old lady cackled. 'Nobody ever comes through here. Essen is the place to look for foreigners. They say there is a black man there. From Egypt, I think they said. Have you tried Essen?'

The lean and dangerous one stirred. He reached into his coat and took out a pistol.

'Where is the girl, Grandma?'

192

'Anna? Couldn't you see she was doing the washing?'

'Show me,' the lean one said.

'Show these gentlemen the wash-house,' Grandma said. 'Then you'll take something to eat with us, I don't doubt. Let me sweep the floor first.'

The three men walked across the yard to a small stone building. Inside, Anna was feeding chips of wood and dried cowpats to a fire burning under an iron tub. The sheets floated in milky water. Wrangl shook his head in disgust and took a swig from the bottle he had snatched up from the kitchen table. Anna offered his companion the dolly stick and he punched down some of the ballooning fabric. His free hand still held the pistol.

'If I thought you were playing the fool with me, any of you, your shitty little lives wouldn't be worth living.'

'Search the barns,' Hans Georg said. 'I don't know why you picked on us but we've done nothing wrong. If you have some quarrel with this Englishman, don't bring it here.'

'What quarrel can we have?' Wrangl asked mildly enough. 'What do you think is happening?'

'Perhaps you are robbers looking for an associate,' Anna suggested.

'Robbers?'

She shrugged. 'Perhaps he has made off with money that belongs to you. We know nothing about things like that.'

'Do we look like robbers to you?'

'I don't know. We are only trying to help you.'

The lean stranger pointed his pistol at the roof and fired. Anna screamed. Both she and her father

193

flung themselves to the dirt floor of the laundry.

'You people ought to be in a zoo,' he said. 'This is not living, what you do here. Dogs lead a better life.'

Following the sound of the shot, a man ran to the courtyard's entrance, an old man with snow-white hair and blue-veined arms. It was Dietze, their neighbour, an interfering fool with one cow and half a hectare of potatoes.

'Help,' he cried. 'Murder!'

He had a peasant's sense of propriety, waving his skinny arms and bellowing but taking care not to cross an imaginary line that ran through the mud and rocks dividing Hans Georg's yard from the rest of the world. The two strangers watched him through a cobwebbed window, shouting and looking this way and that for the help he knew did not exist. The fat man laughed.

'Look at him jig! That is one stupid old bastard.'

The man with the pistol sauntered out of the wash-house, took aim in the most mannered and sardonic way possible and shot him dead. The fat man seized Anna by her hair and dragged her on her knees to Dietze's corpse.

'You have killed him!' she spluttered.

'That was the idea. By way of warning. Tonight we stay in Stoppenberg. If by noon tomorrow we have heard nothing from you, we shall come back and burn this rat's nest to the ground. We are not robbers. We are businessmen.'

'He is in the stable,' Hans Georg called, defeated.

'No!' Anna screamed.

The two Krupp's employees sprinted back across the yard. Hans Georg grabbed his daughter's wrist and ran into the house. Stumbled into the kitchen sobbing with terror. Bolted the door, jagging a flap of skin from his thumb. Turned—and came face to face with a complete stranger, holding his shotgun as if he knew how to use it.

'Cartridges,' Murch said. 'Go and get them. Stay away from the windows. You're a big man, so stop that bloody snivelling.'

'They don't speak English, Billy.'

'They don't need to, Mr Westland,' Murch said, very calm. 'But if you could just convey to this cove that we are up shit alley unless he wakes his ideas up—'

There were plenty of times in the coming months to piece together how, while the men were gassing inside, Anna dragged Philip to a tool shed attached to the house; how Murch, passing at just the right time, heard the shot fired through the laundry roof, jumped the farm wall and came into the house by way of a vegetable garden and narrow back door. How he found the kitchen empty, heard the second shot, saw Dietze's body fall, and then, miraculously, saw the old girl dragging Philip Westland inside by his heels.

'Tell Ma she's a good 'un,' Murch said now, throwing over the oak table and dragging it to the far wall, with just enough space for Philip and the womenfolk to crouch behind. He took off his jacket and hung it absent-mindedly on the back of the last upright chair.

'Now let's get this straight,' he said. 'Those evil bastards outside have already killed. I've arrived a bit tardy and don't have the full story but you can have my word on it that they won't pack up shop and go home. They'll want to come and join us in here. And that ain't going to happen.'

By way of demonstration, the two Krupp's men burst out of the stables in high old mood. When they saw the door to the house closed, they conferred briefly. Inside, Hans Georg passed Murch a battered cardboard box. Lolling in the bottom were just three cartridges. To Billy's eye the brass bases looked suspiciously dull. He touched the breech of the gun and gave its owner an interrogative thumbs-up. Hans Georg nodded.

'Herr Westland,' the fat man called from the yard. 'We know you are in there. Already there has been such unpleasantness. We are not here to kill you but to take you back to Essen. Where everything can be decided in a proper fashion. Like gentlemen. No one will be harmed.'

'You have already killed an innocent man,' Philip shouted.

'No, he was not innocent! As our report shall show. He was assisting you in your attempt to escape. An accomplice, I think.'

'Oh, sod this,' Billy Murch said. He knocked a pane of glass from the window with the muzzle of the shotgun. Saw them flinch and dive behind a cattle trough. Considered a shot and then decided against it.

'Tell them you are not coming out and they are not coming in,' he commanded Philip. 'And best to add, sir, that if they so much as break wind behind that there trough arrangement, I will blow someone's head off. You might mention the notion of a crack shot and so forth.'

'If you come any closer I will kill you,' Philip yelled.

The answer was derisive laughter. Murch fired, just to wipe the smile off their faces. Hitting the trough was no good: he aimed at a lump of rock to one side and shattered it. The fragments sang as they flew.

'Now listen to me, Mr Westland. They are going to rush the house. They don't have any choice—even in this forsaken hole a crowd of witnesses is going to form. They don't want that. When it happens—when they come through that door—this here German bloke will be with you behind the table. He should have one up the spout and the time to let fly is when they're framed in the doorway. Translate.'

Hans Georg listened to Philip with a green face, his head shaking vigorously. For all his size—and his was twice Billy's weight—he was in no mood at all to play the hero. When he was offered the gun, he pushed it back.

'Just what I thought. Tell him to get right out of it, then. He can hide upstairs. If they win down here, he's a dead man anyway. But get him out now. I don't want him in my squad.'

'Give Anna the gun. She'll do it.'

Murch thought about that and then shook his head.

'No. Tell Grandma I need her to do it.'

The old lady's head appeared above the table like a weasel's. Murch smiled encouragingly.

'When she was younger, did she ever fire a rabbit gun?'

'This isn't the Wild West, Billy.'

'Make sure she knows what to do. Frame 'em up in the doorway, then boom! Just point at the open doorway—boom!'

'This man has balls bigger than an ox,' the old lady decided. She wiped her nose with the back of her wrist and held out her hand for the gun.

'Not yet, not yet. Now I want Anna to tell them how no one's listening to you, they're all terrified and they are coming out. And make it convincing.'

As she spoke, Murch ran to the table and passed her grandmother the gun. Then ran back and made a noisy business of drawing the bolts on the door. Pulled the door open slowly, slowly. Whatever the girl was saying, it was impressively passionate. A late addition to the plan: on the wall behind him, Murch found a glass-framed picture of the Lord Jesus Shining His Light unto the World. He took it off its hook and tested it for heft.

'They are standing up,' Philip called softly. 'They are arguing what to do.'

'Tell them that without help, you cannot fight them. You surrender. Beg them to save your life. Pour it on. Loads of gravy.'

And if this isn't the trickiest bit, Billy thought. If they decide to split up we are in trouble. If they don't take the bait at all, I don't have a better idea. Millie, old girl, I may have overreached myself at last.

'They're coming,' Philip called softly. Murch held up two fingers by way of a question. 'Yes,' Philip answered.

'Tell Ma to wait until they're right on the threshold—'

But the two killers had broken into a run. Murch ducked behind the door only a second before the shotgun went off. There was a gasp and an oath, followed by a pistol shot. The air was thick with white powder—the old woman had fired as instructed but missed the target and hit the ceiling, bringing down a shower of laths and perhaps a century of limewash and rat droppings. Billy held the religious print sideways on, stepped out from behind the door and swung the frame like an axe at the man nearest him. It was Wrangl. The blow caught him at eye level across the bridge of his nose and instinctively he turned away, his head in his hands.

In the smother of dust, the lean and dangerous one was cursing and firing his pistol across the kitchen. He turned his head to cope with this unexpected threat from his right—but just a second too late. Billy had changed grip and holding Jesus Shining His Light unto the World like a racquet, smashed it into the killer's face. The glass shattered.

As Billy had learned, having made his way down a long corridor of fights like this in the past, it was not the first blow that counted, but the second, third and fourth. And the trick of that was never to hesitate, never improvise. He was fighting a man with a pistol in his hand who was thrown back on his heels for only a split second. But in that tiny window of time he stepped across the killer's body, grabbed his gun arm high up near the armpit, seized his wrist and turned him against the wall. The German knew what was coming, dipped his shoulder and sank to the floor. It was a defence, he was strong, he held the gun. His elbow joint was intact.

But there exists a visceral understanding in fights, something that comes in well below the level of thought. The German's body was already accepting, on behalf of the brain, that it could not win. Though the two men fought on for another two minutes, the pistol became an irrelevance. To the outsider—to Anna watching in horror from behind the overturned table—the struggle seemed even-handed and the outcome doubtful. When Wrangl staggered back in and knelt beside the writhing figures to beat with his fists on Billy's back, it almost seemed that fortunes had changed. But, for his companion, it was the end. Cramped up by Wrangl's body, he exposed his neck for a fraction of a second too long. The shard of glass in Billy's hand plunged into his carotid artery, producing a fountain of blood. His boots began drumming on the stone-flagged floor.

'Not me, not me,' Wrangl cowered, his soft little hands held against his face.

'Look away,' Billy shouted to the girl.

Then slit the fat man's throat, the way that butchers slaughter pigs. When he stood up, the eye that he caught was Philip Westland's. And if he says anything, I will pick this bloody revolver up and kill the lot of them. Stone me if I ever pull a stroke like this again, Billy thought, wiping his face free of blood and spitting out a tooth. You and me are for some other world, Millie girl, some better place. In future we shall leave the gentlemen to settle their own quarrels. We'll hook ourselves right out of it—I don't say no to a lock-keeper's cottage and a corduroy suit, my oath if I don't. But anyway, far, far away from this.

Grandma floated towards him across the littered floor. She sat him down with his back against the wall, and stroked his face, his hair. Then laid her cheek against his shoulder for a moment. He patted her bony spine, wondering how to ask for coffee in her own lingo.

'Billy?' Westland said quietly. 'We must go home.'

'You won't get an argument from me,' Murch said drily. 'But what say we tidy up a bit first? Dig a deep hole and plant the bodies. Then a doctor for you. I daresay we could use a cart or something of the sort.'

Which is how Pastor Bisblinkoff came to find his yellow and black trap, his pride and joy and one remaining consolation in life, gone, along with Rudi the pony. Christian forgiveness could not answer the situation and when his wife suggested he calm down, he picked a massively heavy bust of Bismarck from the mantelpiece and threw it through the window.

FIFTEEN

Commander Alcock kept a desk at the Admiralty in a section to do with chart revisions, compiled and collated from reports by ships' masters across five oceans. For example, in 1876, the very dubious entrance to Puerto Deseado on the coast of Argentina was compromised by the collision of two merchant vessels just at the narrowest point of entry to the harbour. The wrecks remained unmarked until an apoplectic Captain Pottinger, RN, ran foul of them in the *Acheron*, toppling the smoke stack from his ship, shearing off the propellor and hazarding the lives of 247 men.

Alcock's civilian clerks were meticulous and patient men, none of whom had been to sea

201

themselves. They enjoyed the celestial laughter that hung over some of the reports and signals: it was a pleasure to read as a footnote to Captain Pottinger's misfortunes how the Mayor of Puerto Deseado had shot dead his brother-in-law the harbour master for his dilatoriness in marking the wrecks, 'thus saving their Lordships the trouble of an official censure'. In another ocean altogether, volcanic activity had closed the small trading station at Bintochan on the Sumatra coast, isolating 700 tons of coal that had once stood dockside but was now three miles inland. Stranded along with the coal was a Baptist mission and its next-door neighbour, the notorious Lucky Boy brothel.

Alcock dealt with certain boxes whose contents were examined by his eyes only and filed in a green and gold floor safe to which he had the sole key. It was the Chief Clerk's understanding that what came across the Commander's desk contained information of a sensitive political or diplomatic nature that might not bear directly on revised instructions to mariners. He was content with that, as how could he be otherwise? Alcock, for all his fussy manners and demands to behold a tight ship when he walked into his dusty offices every morning on the stroke of ten, was otherwise the perfect boss. At half past twelve each day, he went to lunch and was not seen again until three and sometimes four in the afternoon.

'Your man had a miserable time of it among the Teutons,' Radley of the Foreign Office observed over lamb cutlets at the Travellers.

'The task was beyond him.'

'Bit harsh, what? Wasn't he shot by some chap

202

supposed to be on our side?'

'It would seem so.'

'Herr Krupp set the dogs on him consequently?'

'You are remarkably well informed.'

'Well, he was trying to make off with what amount to state secrets. We tend to hear about that sort of thing. Do we know where he is now?'

'He managed to find his way to Duisberg and signalled from there that he was taking ship to Rotterdam.'

'When you say "taking ship"—?'

'Taking barge then,' Alcock said, greatly niggled. 'In any case, I do not intend to use him again. He lacks what I call the killer instinct.'

'Poor fellow,' Radley drawled.

'On that subject, did you receive my note on Pottinger?'

'Remind me.'

'Captain, RN.'

'The man who tried to start a war with Argentina.'

'You are very facetious,' Commander Alcock complained testily. 'The incident at Puerto Deseado was the only blemish on an otherwise impeccable record. Captain Pottinger has since resigned the service.'

'How did that go down with their Lordships?' Radley asked, who knew the answer.

'He is headstrong, I grant you. But I believe I can find him work.'

'Has he the killer instinct?'

'Great heavens, yes!' Alcock exclaimed, as though his companion had just asked the most redundant question possible. 'When he was a midshipman in the *Amphytriton*, he picked up a fractious mule in Valetta one afternoon and flung it bodily into the sea. A twenty-stone *mule.*'

'I did not know that,' Radley murmured. 'So Westland will give way to this fellow, is that it?'

'That is the plan.'

Lucky Westland, Radley thought, stirring the peas on his plate and wondering—not for the first time—whether there was a Mrs Alcock; and if so, what she found to console herself with in what was a very common sort of villa on Battersea Rise.

'Does your man speak a language?' he asked absent-mindedly.

'Welsh,' Alcock said, after a slight pause.

                    *   *   *

'If you ask me,' Charlie MacGill observed, 'your fellow was very lucky to have had you by him.'

'I didn't ask you,' Billy Murch replied. The little Scots engineer nodded. No offence taken. The two men sat on kitchen chairs on the afterdeck of the Dutch tug, watching the barge train strung out behind. It was night, and they were passing a small town on the German side of the Rhine, distinguished by a few strings of street lights. The only signs of life on the barges were washing lines and the sparks from galley chimneys. The very, very faint strains of an accordion—the sailor's piano—drifted down on them from the second boat in line.

'A hunting accident, you said,' MacGill prompted.

'Would you be a nosy bugger at all?'

'Not specially. I'm from Greenock, me. That's a Willis and Simms engine you hear down below.

Not exactly the state of the art but I can claim to know it as well as the man who made the first drawings. Aye, I keep that pile of shite as fine-tuned as any concert violin. And to mark your card for you, Jimmy, what we are doing here is drinking my beer and making conversation.'

Properly rebuked, Billy rolled MacGill a cigarette and passed it across.

'He's had a bit of bad luck,' he said. 'I came to fetch him home. Reckoned a bed in this old tub better than a train ride any day of the week. Give his wound a chance to heal.'

'That would be right,' MacGill agreed. 'The pair of you master and servant, no doubt.'

'That sort of thing.'

'Aye, aye,' the engineer said musingly. 'Weel, as I say, he's lucky to have you by him. And what did you make of the German laddies you met with?'

'A bit on the slow side?' Billy suggested. MacGill struck his thigh in delight.

'Are they not! But terrible swift to take offence, wouldn't you say?'

'You've had dealings with them, have you?'

'Good God, man, am I not married to a Rhine maiden? Calm enough she is, the great lummox, as big in the beam as one of yon barges. A floating island, you might say. But her brother is a different proposition altogether. A frown on him enough to frighten horses.'

'There have had to be words with the cove from time to time,' Billy guessed. MacGill laughed and lobbed his beer bottle into the glassy river.

'You'd know all about that,' he said with Greenock shrewdness. 'We'll fetch to Rotterdam about three tomorrow. The Harwich ferry sails at

205

seven. It's been a pleasure talking with you, sonny.'

He dropped through an open hatch to where the Willis and Simms chuntered in a fine mist of oil, every bit of brasswork, every copper tube polished up like Rob Roy's dinner service. Billy groped about in the thrumming dark and opened the door to Philip Westland's berth, finding an impossibly narrow bunk and a further four feet by nine of free space. Every inch of wall was taken up by hooks, or at any rate the clothes they supported. The triumphantly oily smell of MacGill's engines was mingled with more familiar stinks—sweat, sausage and onions, tar and canvas, tobacco.

Philip was awake. The bandage that the Duisberg doctor had applied glowed in the dark, possibly the whitest and cleanest thing ever seen in this cabin. He held out his hand to Billy with a wry smile.

'This is all very cosy,' he murmured weakly. 'Where do you sleep tonight?'

'On the floor here, I fancy.'

'You were a good man to come and find me, Billy.'

'It was nothing.'

'Well, no, it was quite a lot. I think you dug the graves of three people.'

'Shots were exchanged,' Murch allowed in his characteristically flat way. But Philip was thinking more of the sound a throat makes when it is slit from ear to ear; and the drumming of heels on a stone floor.

'I'll not put you to such trouble again,' he said— and hated himself for such an insipid and cowardly way of expressing thanks. 'This is my last excursion, I promise you.'

'What will you do?'

'Marry Bella. Mrs Wallis, that is.'

'I am very pleased to hear it.'

'You think I will make her happy?'

Murch was always a bit niggardly when it came to smiles but he bestowed one on Philip now that would have melted the polar ice cap.

'Never a dull moment between the pair of you,' he promised. 'Never a moment's regret, never a backward glance.'

'You sent her the telegraph?' Philip asked, suddenly anxious.

'All taken care of.'

'And you said nothing in it to alarm her?'

'Never in life.'

*   *   *

Bella had Billy's cable in her hand at breakfast that same morning. It read:

Everything tip-top considering. Weather rainy. On way home. Kind regards. Philp.

'And isn't that the news you've been waiting for?' Dora Venn exclaimed in delight.

'Philip didn't write this.'

'It's good enough for me,' Mrs Venn said. 'A leg of lamb, I think, for when he gets back; and a dish Mrs Bardsoe was mentioning, of summer fruits done up in a pudding. Unless you've got your own ideas, of course.'

'These are not words and expressions Mr Westland might use,' Bella repeated.

'The sense is clear enough, though. Now, I don't

think he will want to find a moping woman when he steps through that door. I shall have Mrs Poe's daughter round to help me buff up this old place and it wouldn't harm to send the girl across to the Garden for an armful of flowers neither. But it will be *your* radiance that cheers his heart.'

Bella studied the cable form more closely. 'Where is Duisburg?' she asked.

'One place much the same as another over there,' Dora Venn declared. A joke occurred to her. 'I don't suppose they know where they are neither! The man to ask would be Charlie Urmiston. There's not a lot gets past him. A regular brainbox when it comes to where things are. Also the kings and queens of England, though that don't come into it in this particular case.'

She is trying to cheer me up, Bella thought when she was finally left alone. The conversation with Sir Edward in Fracatelli's had led to some very untoward behaviour and in consequence several instances of lips pursed and eyebrows raised from Mrs Venn. At first Bella kept to the house, not even venturing as far as Mr Liddell's for a cake, or a bag of his croissants. But yesterday she had spent a small fortune driving about the West End hoping to catch a glimpse of Ursula Gollinge. It was a deeply irrational impulse. She had the cab go up and down Regent Street twice (twice!) and into Piccadilly via Sackville Street. Thence all the way along the south side of the Park, up through Church Street and back down the Bayswater Road.

'Oxford Street or Park Lane?' the veteran cabbie called.

'Would you pull up and talk to me for a moment?' Bella asked.

'Talk to you?' the man said, greatly scandalised. 'I'd as soon drop you off and be done with it. Talk to you! This is a new one and no error. I took you for a lady, missus.'

Which was how she came to walk from Lancaster Gate all the way back to Piccadilly. Trees did not help; Speke's Monument (which she had not previously known to exist) did not help either. She sat on a bench with her back to the Serpentine and astonished herself by weeping.

Look at it this way, Margam said. You—let us call you Lady Barbara Collins—spend a fruitless afternoon in searching for your bitter rival, Ursula Lapointe. Then, just as you are passing the monument to Speke, you see a white carnation laid on its topmost step. You investigate: there is a card. The handwriting is Lapointe's! But does it pay tribute to the great explorer? It does not. It reads, simply, *Ce soir à vingt heures*. (The ink is violet, I fancy.) Suddenly the whole mystery explains itself. This is a blackmail note addressed to your fiancé, Roderick Northland; for Lapointe has discovered that it was he, acting upon orders from the Admiralty, who shot dead John Hanning Speke—

'Oh, for God's sake,' Bella said aloud, disgusted.

If she could see Roderick Northland now, walking towards her across Kensington Gardens with his familiar clumsy gait and lopsided grin, these tears would turn to joy and Ursula Lapointe could go jump in the lake, taking Henry Ellis Margam with her. But the only person walking towards her was an elderly drunk with a sandwich board round his neck reading 'SEEK AND YE SHALL FIND'. He was saved from a kicking by

209

falling over before he could reach her.

*   *   *

The same morning Bella's enigmatic telegram was delivered, Mrs Bardsoe made an excursion to Chiswick by bus and Shanks's pony. Her purpose was only partly charitable. From time to time it did a body good to get out into the fresh air and though she would never admit to being bored by Charles Urmiston, the earnest side of him could grate, occasionally. Across the river was about as far as she would like to go but she enjoyed stomping along, bad knee or not, in what she thought of as foreign parts. She had a very pleasant conversation with a postman and a rather more guarded one with a clerical gentleman in a white straw hat.

And here she was, sitting with Millie Rogerson in the kitchen of the Kennetts' house, her boots off, reading Murch's second telegram from Duisburg, the message to his wife. It read, in its entirety, *Tiddly pom pom pom Murchie*, and Millie was so enchanted that Hannah Bardsoe forgot her aching feet and laughed along with the girl.

'Now my Charlie says there's many a message sent in code and I daresay this is such a one. And where's he been to send you a billy doo like this?'

'"*Tiddly pom pom pom*" says "You'll do for me", Mrs B. And he talks to the baby with those same words. You know,' Millie added shyly, touching her bump.

'Yes, but where's he been?'

'I don't see as how it harms to tell you. He's been to fetch Mr Westland out of a spot of bother

210

in Germany.'

'Oh my lord,' Hannah exclaimed. She had a vague image of endless forests and the long snouts of wolves. 'Whatever was that good man doing poking about out there? He hasn't the brains he was born with, sometimes. And leaving Mrs Wallis to be snatched from the jaws of death in Yorkshire! I tell you, Millie, us women are going to have to put our foot down. I've had Charlie sneezing enough to blow a body's hat off, not to say waking up in a muck sweat babbling about naked women.'

'Go on!' Millie exclaimed in delight.

'As true as I'm sat here. So if your Billy comes home with some of the same ideas, you know where to come.'

'Murchie would run a mile from a naked woman, you can have my word on that. He's as chaste as a pineapple in that respect.'

'And ain't I pleased to hear it. Now before I set off for the omnibus to come here, I walked down the market and bought us both a bit of fish. So do you sit quiet, you beautiful creature, and let old Bardsoe cook you a nice dinner.'

'You don't have to,' Millie protested.

'Well, I know I don't have to.' A thought occured to her. 'One more thing about these men of ours. The problem is, they're all in love with Mrs Wallis without knowing it. And she, poor creature, wandering about like Little Bo Peep. Not that I don't love her dearly myself.'

'It's London,' Millie said. 'It's that what's turned their heads. Rogerson, when he was alive, used to hang about the gates to the Palace, just on the off-chance that he'd be there when the old Queen came to her senses and pitched up back home.'

'Fat chance of that!'

'That's what I used to tell him. And that she aren't no more a Londoner than Garibaldi or one of that lot. But he would have none of it. He wanted to be there when Her Majesty leaned out of her coach and said, "Bobby, I've done this old city wrong, but I've seen the errors of my ways. Bring your pals round for a drink, why don't you?"'

'You say it's London: I say it's Bella Wallis.'

Millie laughed and jumped up to help Mrs Bardsoe light the range, which could be a bit tricky on a windless day. (The flue had been modified by her employer William Kennett, along rational lines, one lazy afternoon a year or so ago. Except in gale conditions, it had never worked properly since.)

'I will say this. Mrs Wallis is the biggest Londoner of them all. And that's why they love her.'

'Even Mr Kennett?'

'Oh,' Millie cried delightedly. 'Now there's a man who lives out among the fairies. We can't bring him into it. You want to hear Murchie on that subject.'

'And what does he say?'

'That he is Mary Kennett's humming bird.'

*   *   *

The Hooterville Assay Office was a clapboard building painted battleship grey. Next door to it a grandson of the original Hooter kept a dry goods store and general chandlery. There were another five businesses and then the smudged valleys of that part of California began, the home to snakes, wild dogs, rats and a handful of leathery men with spades and tents. Hooterville had no church, no doctor and only an intermittent supply of beer and whiskey. Old Henry Hooter had planted a few lemon trees at the back of his property and these provided the signature luxury of this little nightmare community—Ma Hooter's Lemon Barley. It was served in half-pint jugs at five cents a throw, ten with a jigger of corn whiskey added.

The assay office had of course no connections to the American Mint. Its existence was entirely cosmetic, a honey trap to lure dude prospectors such as William and Mary Kennett. Its manager was a man called John Joseph Beaminster, recruited by the Hooter family to add a little gloss to the idea that this was a gold town. Had anyone ever come off the hills with a strike worth more than a few flakes, the nearest official assay office was to be found in Idaho, where the premises were three storeys high and staffed by federal employees in wing collars.

The Hooters came originally from Illinois; Mr Beaminster was the last of five generations of Dorset folk who had blown like dandelion seed across America. In 1790, Jethro Smalls had changed his name to Beaminster in honour of the town where his grandfather was born. It was not a popular gesture, especially among barefoot neighbours who were called Scroggs, Shinner, Bluett or Raikes. But it had produced, after a succession of daydreamers, John Joseph, a reading man and halfway to being a gentleman. Just what he was doing swatting flies in Hooterville he left others to ponder. He liked the Kennetts for never asking.

'Ahah!' Beaminster exclaimed in kindly fashion to William. 'More rocks for me to look at! Not that I would rather cast my eye upon the only truly priceless nugget in these here miserable surroundings. I speak of Mrs Kennett.'

'She is in Hooter's, buying some bacon slab and drinking a lemon barley.'

'I knew that particular pig,' John Joseph quipped merrily. 'As good-natured an animal as ever walked. And hasn't the pig been as much a friend to this nation as the Constitution itself? If there is anything more toothsome than a gammon steak with a garnish of wild mushrooms, I should like to hear of it, sir.'

'I pine for a sirloin of beef, all the same,' Kennett admitted.

'It is the Englishman in you! No doubt you live in a castle back home. This must seem a far cry indeed from those native shores. A castle, and maybe as many as ten or fifteen gardeners. You have heard of Parnham House, I don't doubt?'

'I'm afraid not. In Dorset, that would be.'

When he first met Beaminster, William Kennett supposed him to be touched by the sun; or maybe congenitally damaged in some way or other. It took him a while to realise that his friend was simply bored and thus more often than not drunk. Later still, he learned that Beaminster was writing a history of his ancestral birthplace, derived from family legend. Central to the story was how the Smalls, as they were then, had lent money to the beardless youth Thomas Hine to find his way to France and so found (in a revolutionary year) Cognac Hine on the banks of the Charente at a place called Jarnac. The place name rang no bells with William Kennett and the point of Beaminster's book was to point out that a loan made in 1788 had by now accrued enough interest to change the scenery of his own life in a quite spectacular way.

'I admire you, Mr Kennett, I surely do. You are a man after my own heart, sir, a dreamer of dreams. Would it be impudent of me to describe you as a shameless romantic?'

He leaned forward with a leer and lowered his voice to a friendly whisper.

'I see you are packing iron, as they say out here. Now is that pistol and gunbelt a way of tipping your cap to the legendary West at all? Or does it, as we might say, lend a little local colour to your prospecting endeavours?'

'It is no more than a sensible precaution, Mr Beaminster, in the circumstances.'

'And what circumstances might those be?'

William hoisted his sack of finds onto the table between them. When Beaminster tipped out the contents, he rose, pushed back his chair and howled like a prairie dog. The dude, God blind his eyes, had struck it rich. Not just a little bit rich but filthily richer than the most leather-necked veteran could ever envisage.

'Do you know what you have here, sir?'

'Well, yes,' William Kennett murmured with his trademark shyness, indicating that Beaminster should return the nuggets to the sack and then the sack to its owner. The American fell to his knees and beat his head on the rough-hewn floor.

'If this don't beat all in the story of my miserable unhappy life,' he sobbed.

215

'Take heart,' William said. 'Come and have a lemon barley. But of course, if you blab one word to that swindling rascal Hooter, I shall have to shoot you. If you keep calm then we can surely find a way to make you rich—not unfeasibly rich but as we say in our English castle, comfy.'

'Comfy? That's a word?'

'My wife swears by it. And she is trying to persuade me to trust you.'

'Tell me what to do! Ask me for anything.'

'Well, it's like this. I never expected to find any gold. Now that I have, I don't know what to do with it.'

'You sell it,' Beaminster yelled, beside himself. 'Are you a goddamn idiot, sir? Are you *drunk*?'

'I am on my honeymoon,' William Kennett said rather stiffly. His own opinion of Mr Beaminster was far less flattering than his wife's. But then Mary had shown herself to be a shrewd judge of the American character—and so it proved to be in this instance. All Beaminster had ever wanted from life was for someone to love him and once he had that, he blossomed into the business manager from heaven.

SIXTEEN

Six months passed. How easy to say, as though clocks ticked, the sun rose and set, rain turned to sleet and then snow, coal was shovelled recklessly in parlours from Stepney to Shepherd's Bush, bringing in its wake the London fog, yellow and brown as dog fur—and all this as ordinary as

216

teacups. But in these particular six months, Murch was presented with a daughter; William and Mary Kennett returned from America as proprietors of the Lucky Buckaroo gold mine; the boy Alfie Stannard was brought down from Yorkshire and set up in a tiny business selling not sweets but stamp packets for child collectors, a trade he adored. Percy Quigley came across (in his usual way of coming across things) enough tongue-and-groove boarding to refit the offices in Fleur de Lys Court as handsomely as any solicitor's—if the right person could be found to talk an innocent in to doing it for nothing. Equally amazing in its own quiet way, Charles Urmiston grew a beard to rival the Prince of Wales's—grey, close-trimmed and with the same elegant tip.

Two things did not happen. Ursula Gollinge, if she really was in London, did not show her face, not so much as a glimpse. And Bella Wallis did not marry Philip Westland.

'If I normally walked on my hands, these trips would be the very thing to help recuperate a shoulder wound,' he complained as they paid their second winter visit to Brighton. 'But staggering about on the shingle here is doing very little for me.'

'Not very adventurous, I grant you.'

'Could we at least go somewhere where the sea is green? Better still, blue.'

'We are here for the air,' Bella chided. 'There are poor devils sticking pigs in Poona who would give their eye teeth for a bucket of this sleet.'

They kissed. No danger of compromising their dignity: the winter beaches were empty of everything but themselves and a raging squall.

Driftwood and scraps of kelp flew past their heads. Out to sea, the sky was flecked by seagulls yet to make landfall on the town's roofs.

'We can go for a cup of tea now,' Bella decided.

Their failure to crown a dangerous and reckless summer by marrying was exercising everyone, though Hannah Bardsoe thought she had an explanation. As lovers (and what could be more romantic than the two of them tucked up in Orange Street, like sparrows squabbling under the eaves one day, cooing like vicarage doves the next?) they thought too much. Thinking was all very well in its way and folk had a right to carry on as they pleased, but in love too much brains could be as dangerous as too little. To see Bella in her edgiest moods was a sorry trial to the roly-poly Hannah and her own plain and straightforward way of going on. Being *clever* about love was utterly foreign to her nature. She would as soon believe in unicorns wandering out of the forests to lay their heads in a maiden's lap.

'I'm sure you've never looked at me in that light,' she challenged Charles Urmiston.

'In what light is that?' he asked cautiously.

'Like a bit of long division,' she explained, stunning him by the simile. 'Or anything else of that nature. Sums, I mean.'

'I think of you as my favourite prime number,' he protested. As a gallantry, it fell flat. Indeed, Hannah bristled.

'I was hoping for remarks pertinent and not some beardie nonsense.'

'Well, how about this? Certainly they love each other to distraction. Yet there is some small thing between those two admirable people that has yet to be resolved before they marry. Some final sticking point. If you like, a pea under their mattress.'

'Rubbish.'

'Just as you say.'

'Sticking point! They are made for each other, those two, as anyone can see. Why, 'tis plain as a pikestaff, Charlie. Unless—'

'Unless what?'

She was going to say that they—the two of them, along with Quigley and Billy Murch—might be just too much for Philip Westland to stomach any more. It was in her mind that both lovers had come up against the jaws of death in recent times, only to be saved (once again) by others. It did not seem like the recipe for a happy marriage. Hannah set great store in her own life by untroubled ordinariness. Confronted in the shop by some growth or swelling, perhaps some rash that ran red as raspberry jam across a shyly presented belly, she was worth any amount of pills to the worried patient.

'Ho! That's nothing very much! Didn't your neighbour Mrs Potts have the same? And isn't she still scrubbing out the Eagle Insurance at six every morning? Which I see her passing home when I takes down the shutters, as blithe as a cricket, always a kind word.'

Her beloved Charlie sometimes said she was a bit too free with her diagnoses but then he came out of the same box as Bella and could not be expected to understand that many of their customers could not afford a doctor and believed (rightly) that a turn in a charity hospital was as good as kissing the world goodbye. What they wanted from Hannah was the reassurance that nothing was so bad it could not be endured. Philip Westland, for all that he'd gone off to Germany on some unexplained jaunt and got himself shot, was Hannah's idea of a philosophical cove at heart, much in her own pattern. If you didn't like the way things were turning out, you had to learn to lump it. Bella was different.

'There is always someone riding to the rescue with her,' she muttered. Urmiston's sharp glance made her blush.

'Hark at me,' she exclaimed guiltily. 'What do I know about anything, a fat old body no taller than a Shetland pony?'

'Mmm,' Urmiston teased. 'You make a good point there, my precious.'

His beard was prickly but, at close range, comforting. Best of all, it did not smell of tobacco or stale soap but rather (though very faintly) of cough syrup, something they had begun to manufacture out in the kitchen and which flew off the shelves, people coming from as far as Southwark to buy it in the trademark red bottle. She sat on his lap, consenting to be kissed.

'You'd never leave me, Charlie?'

'The little Bienkowski girl came into the shop yesterday. I have always thought of her as very pretty. Well formed and so forth.'

'Oh, I daresay it will come to that one day. That's a story about men, not her and her kind, the impudent little cat. And good luck to you, for she'll leave you as skinned as a rabbit when she's had her fill of you. But you'd never leave me, all the same?'

'Never in life,' he promised. 'As if you don't know.'

There *was* a sticking point in Bella's relationship with Philip and it had to do with Ursula Gollinge. For it did not take much detective work from Bella to confirm that it was this vile woman who had undone Jane Westland twelve years earlier. Had she never gone to Yorkshire, Philip would have kept his silence, for just as Bella had nothing to say about her first marriage and subsequent affaire with the elfin Marie Claude, so he censored anything to do with the time before Bella. This reticence was simply a matter of form. Neither of them believed in love as an interrogation.

What came out of the past came unbidden; and as often as not, wearing an antic mask. So it was that Bella knew of the sixteen-year-old Philip being seduced by a much older woman in Florence; an ancient infatuation that had turned by now to moth-eaten farce. Likewise—because it was much in her mind after the sculptor's death—she told him the story of defending herself with a broom in Musgrave's studio, without mentioning that she was at the time stark naked save for a chaplet of laurel. (Nor that the broom came into the story as a late—a very late—rush of common sense after an afternoon's reckless flirting.)

Such episodes from the past flitted in and out of their pillow conversations without causing the slightest harm. They were shameless for the very reason that some dreams are shameless: they came from a place that has no real geography, where mirrors reflect back nothing but smoke. They were remembered only because they had been so long

221

forgotten.

'What made you think of your Florentine adventure tonight?' Bella asked when she was first told of the voracious seductress of the Villa Danielli.

'I was just thinking vaguely about how hopeless I am at undressing in front of anyone,' Philip confessed, sending his beloved Bella into hoots of laughter.

Ursula Gollinge was a different matter. It was as if her burly, thuggish persona could never become anything whimsical and dreamlike. The reason was of course unfinished business, located in Jarnac, where Jane Westland languished.

'It is now or never, Philip,' she whispered one night. 'If we don't bring this into the open, it will poison everything between us for ever.'

'There are parts to the story I have never been able to tell you. Things that might hurt you.'

'Nothing you can say will harm me, Philip,' Bella said. And then for a long time there was silence, save for the rain in the gutters. She had a reasonable idea of the details he wished to keep from her but had the sense to keep quiet. He threw the covers off and got out of bed to watch the rain patter up and down the pavements, his cheek against the window glass.

'She was an incredibly gifted child,' he began. 'My mother died in having her and my father brought us up with the aid of governesses and the like. We were hardly affected by having only one parent, perhaps because my father was the most phlegmatic man in Christendom. As children we lived in Oxfordshire on a little island of wealth and security. I am far more of a country mouse than

I've ever told you, Bella.'

'And Jane?'

'The same. We lived like savages, built treehouses, swam in the lake, slept outdoors.'

'But your father kept up a house in London?'

'In Dalmire Gardens. He gave dinners for his antiquarian colleagues and kept most of his books there. We went for walks, sailed on the river to Greenwich and suchlike, haunted museums and galleries. We were a very close-knit family. And horribly priggish into the bargain. But what we knew about life—or thought we knew—was all hidden away behind elms and attended by skylarks. London was—' he hesitated—'less real.'

She thought about that. For her the city was everything, all the more alluring for being so difficult to master. London was the conversation that one never tired of having, the table that was constantly being relaid.

'I am cold,' Philip said suddenly. 'Could we go down and perhaps rekindle the fire? Take a little brandy together?'

It was half past one in the morning when they tiptoed downstairs, a dangerous time for letting truth slip the leash and run free. They sat in the dark at opposite sides of the hearth, watching the fresh coals fume.

'You have to think of Jane as bearing the burden of impossible expectations. My father wanted a consort, I suppose. At the back of his mind he saw Jane alongside him in the house at Radcot, enjoying a summer's day that would last until his death. She was not to change her character to accommodate him, nor suffer by the arrangement in any way. She would grow from a girl to a woman

223

in his company and some magic or other would supply a happy outcome.'

'Instead, she ran away,' Bella divined.

'The first time when she was seventeen. We found her in Chelsea, living with a bachelor friend of my father's. Under his roof, that is, for the poor old man had as much need of a woman in the house as he might have for a pig, or a penfold of sheep. On the advice of an incredibly stupid doctor, my father took her to Bad Gastein for the waters. There she was seduced by an American woman. Is seduced the right word?'

'Please, Philip,' Bella whispered.

'I told you there were things you might not wish to hear. There was nothing physical about the relationship, I am sure. Jane simply ran about after this poor woman, much as a small child at a wedding pesters a glamorous guest. She ambushed her at breakfast, contrived to join her for walks and excursions—that sort of thing.'

He fell silent for a few moments, a picture of unhappiness.

'The hotel was a small one. There were letters and poems, all of which the American bore with good grace. I have tried to imagine it a hundred times, Bella—this glorious young woman in a white gown, searching and calling under the lanterns that lit the gardens—'

Bella jumped up and sloshed cognac into her glass, weeping tears that ran along the line of her chin. In the darkness, Philip sighed defeatedly.

'No,' she said sharply. 'I want to hear it all.'

'There are people who go to spas for nothing else but gossip. What greater topic than this wild swan of a girl making a fool of herself? Only after

224

it was all over did I meet the American. She was an extremely intelligent woman and I think a good one. It was years later and we met completely by accident in Rome. She remembered Jane and asked after her with great tenderness. She was the first to suggest that my sister's troubles were deeper seated than we imagined. I am trying to be fair, Bella.'

'You are trying to avoid saying that you and your father believed she could change her nature if she wanted to. That she would learn to grow up. Isn't that the phrase for it?'

'I am trying to tell you that this girl, whom I adored, for whom I would willingly have given my own life, as being the better bargain, was already as unhappy as anyone I have ever met. To want happiness for another person and not to be able to provide it is a shattering thing.'

'Your father took her out of Germany?'

'He had no choice. He moved permanently to London in an attempt to bring her out into society. There were more scandals. He died in 1865 of a sudden stroke and the day of the funeral, Jane threw herself under a train at Baker Street. The carriages passed completely over her. Standing on the platform was Ursula Gollinge.'

Philip threw his glass into the fire and the cognac in it ignited in a blossom of blue flame that made them both start.

'I am sorry,' he said in a broken voice, 'but I am going to dress and walk somewhere, to the river, perhaps. I can't stay here.'

'I will come with you.'

In the end they walked down Whitehall and up Victoria Street; thence, more or less aimlessly into

225

Belgravia. The rain had stopped and they walked arm in arm, moving from pool to pool of lamplight, sometimes down tunnels of dark. The gutters ran black.

'Jane's American friend was very rich, very cultured. There was a calmness about her, a civility if you like. She was quite small, extremely fastidious in how she dressed, unsmiling, and I suppose the word is imperturbable. Maybe she was forty, maybe sixty. Who could say—and what did it matter?'

Bella suddenly tightened her grip on his arm. Thirty yards in front of them, a fox pattered up from a basement area and stood regarding them. Its coat was not sleek, but stirred up by the rain. It turned away and then looked over its shoulder one last time before trotting away towards Knightsbridge and the Park.

'A *fox*,' Bella whispered. 'How is that possible?'

'What is not possible in London?' Philip muttered.

The rest of the story came out in slow bursts, as though Westland had it all in his head as one continuous narrative but was editing it out of compassion for his lost sister.

Ursula Gollinge had organised Jane's release from underneath the train and whisked her away before the police arrived. They went to a hotel in York Terrace and hid there the rest of the afternoon. Later, a house in Marchmont Street.

'Gollinge was newly arrived from Australia and already notorious. The mad-doctors had taken her husband and she herself was without money or connections of any kind. No house in London would receive her. God knows what Jane thought about any of this. Hotels, rented cottages, even uninvited appearances at country-house weekends. There was family of some kind in Ireland and they made a half-hearted attempt to flee there. They got as far as Liverpool.'

'How do you know this?'

'There were letters to the house in Dalmire Gardens. Not from Jane, not a word from Jane, ever. But Gollinge had a taste for fire-and-brimstone denunciation. One of the packets we received was a missive thirty-seven pages long.'

'Did you employ a detective?'

'A man called Warrender, an Australian who claimed to know her. That might even have been true. But in the end she tired of us. I believe the Queen began to feel the heat of Gollinge's rants. The Queen, the Archbishop of Canterbury, Mr Gladstone. Dr Grace we know about,' he added bitterly.

'Did you know about the curse on Grace when you invited him to dinner?'

'Of course not! Do you think I am mad? I have spent the last ten years trying to obliterate the memory of Ursula Gollinge and all her stupidities.'

'And Jane, all this while the rants and curses were flying?'

'I cannot say,' Philip said. 'But somehow it ended. Her saviour and benefactress found someone else less difficult to command, perhaps. Or—and I would like to believe this—less honest.'

'But a curse was laid on her, all the same?'

Philip sighed. He took Bella in his arms and kissed her cheeks, her forehead.

'What does that really mean, though? She was cursed the very moment she was rescued by

227

Gollinge at Baker Street. I found her in these same streets we have been walking, dressed in rags, begging for food. Would you come to Belgravia for such a thing? But she was like the fox, Bella. She lived in the Park. Ask your question.'

'Don't do this to yourself,' Bella begged, her voice as quiet as the empty streets.

'There is only one question—what did I do about it? I had her back, so what did I do? The answer is, I made just about every mistake a human nonentity could make. She needed a hero. She got me. And an asylum in Charente.'

They walked to Victoria and found a cab.

'Must a man always be a hero?' Bella sobbed.

'Hush,' Philip Westland said. 'Hush, hush.'

SEVENTEEN

Alfie Stannard had been offered lodgings with Charles and Hannah when he first came down from Yorkshire but had the good sense to refuse, finding a place of his own in a lodging house in Eagle Street. He had a single room in the fourth-floor attics and apart from the attentions of a lonely sous-chef, there he found the London he was looking for. It was a sparrow's-eye view of the city, for though his single sash window was small, it overlooked a forest of chimney pots and slate roofs stretching back across Holborn towards the river. This high up, even rain had its own beauty. He rose early every day and was rewarded on Christmas morning by a blood-red dawn, refracted through his iced-over window panes. He had not been slow in picking up the London gift for hyperbole and counted it the finest thing he had ever seen.

'You are very easy pleased,' his neighbour the sous-chef grumbled, patting him on the knee the while. They shared half a bucket of coal and the chef, who was called Arthur and came from Wolverhampton, showed him how to cook steak-and-kidney pie, using scraps of cardboard as examples of the ingredients.

As for the stamp trade, was there anything more romantic in the world? A rich collector might sit at his occasional table in smoking jacket and decorated slippers, poring over his treasures through a cloud of latakia from his meerschaum pipe; but Alfie was at the sharp end of the business, tramping the streets and begging banks and offices to give up their unwanted envelopes, wheedling clerks and junior partners, charming post rooms. It soon enough occurred to him that it was for this he had been set down on earth.

'It seems to me you have gone stamp-mad,' Arthur quipped, peering at him through the magnifying lens, his eye as huge and wet as an oyster.

Hatton Garden was a rich source of postal treasures. The diamond merchant Gorney took a shine to Alfie and passed on stamps from Holland, France and Germany. His more miserly colleague Steinitz struck a stiff price for a small suitcase of similar material that he had intended to study himself (or so he said). Alfie saw the whole trade as hunter-gathering. For him, stamp collecting was done on the hoof, almost as a form of postal delivery in reverse. There was no better way to get to know London at street level and he became a part of the tide that flowed and ebbed along the main thoroughfares and lapped secretly in half-forgotten alleyways.

When he was not searching for the raw materials of his business, he was hawking his made-up penny packets to toy shops, stationers and the bigger traders. The first Stanley Gibbons catalogue was now twelve years old and though stamps were printed in their millions, the chase for rarities had begun. So it was that already some waterholes had run dry, so to speak—the big dealers were there ahead of him in search of varieties. But Alfie worked on the principle that he would rather have three grubby stamps than one perfect example. Soon enough, one wall of the attic was stacked high with boxes and cartons.

He dressed very smartly for a youth of his age, was almost excessively polite to his superiors, did not smoke or drink, and lived for the most part on air. On Sundays he was summoned by Hannah Bardsoe to a roast dinner and plum pudding, an invitation he dared not refuse. After eating up as bidden, he and Charles Urmiston would sit either side of the parlour grate, talking men's talk, as Hannah liked to put it, while she went upstairs for a bit of a lie-down.

On a particular Sunday in March, when even in the sooty canyon that was Shelton Street, spring was announcing itself by some very mild weather indeed, Urmiston found the boy unusually reticent. Conversation about stamps languished and he could not be drawn out on whether he had found himself a young lady (a subject that fascinated Hannah and that Charles had been secretly instructed to enquire about).

'Your mind is elsewhere, Alfie,' Urmiston smiled. 'Last week you were all on fire in finding the four issues of the Danube Steam Ship Company—was it?—in Steinitz's suitcase.'

'Oh, and don't he wish he'd paid more attention to those items when he first came by them,' Alfie responded. But the tone was listless.

'You have had them valued?'

'I was going to ask you to act as my intromederary in that matter, so's not to tip my hand to Mr Gibbon direct.'

'I can see the sense in that,' Urmiston said, after a slight pause. 'But if they are worth what you think they are, shouldn't that be a cause for celebration? If this is your first big coup, why such a long face?'

'I was in Cock Lane on Thursday,' the boy said. 'And I saw someone. Someone you and me thought we would never meet again.'

*   *   *

Urmiston's note was to Philip Westland but in the event both he and Bella came. The five of them sat down to a council of war, Hannah Bardsoe tending the teapot and pressing toasted cheese on everyone, her idea of a Sunday afternoon snack. Alfie was taken through his story for the third time.

'And you can start by explaining why you left it until today to tell anyone about this here encounter,' Hannah chided. 'And only now because your pal Mr Urmiston winkled it out of you, you foolish boy.'

231

'Winkled is a bit strong,' Charles Urmiston protested. 'Our friend was quite properly in two minds what to do. Let him tell the story his own way, Hannah.'

'Let us be free and easy,' Bella agreed, hardly aware of the effect these words had on the still lovelorn Alfie.

'You had to have been there,' he explained.

'Yes, and isn't that always the way?' Bella agreed blithely, compounding the boy's embarrassment. He could not be aware that she too was secretly wracked: she was there to prevent Philip from doing something silly. By which she meant dangerous. Alfie sighed.

'Not much of a story. Either she had been in the pubs or she was took with some of her Yorkshire visions—any road up, she were making a bit of a spectacle of herself. And some.'

Cock Lane a short street, as agreed by all, and Alfie had recognised her the moment he stepped into it. She was wearing a long mauve cloak and a felt hat that was daffodil yellow. The corkscrew curls were uncombed and two savage lines had appeared either side of her nostrils, dragging down her lips. His first reaction on seeing her was one of pity. That took some explaining to Hannah Bardsoe.

'When I lived in Skipton, like, there was an old fighting dog, a bull mastiff that used to hang around the market. He was a famous enough dog in his day but all his real strength was gone. He just *looked* a dangerous beast. That was all that was left to him, you understand. The look of him.'

'And Lady Gollinge affected you in the same way?' Philip prompted gently.

232

'It was a shock. I think I felt a bit of shame, even.'

'Ho, shame! And whatever can that mean when it's at home?' Hannah wanted to know. 'Her as wanted to kill Mrs Wallis and by all accounts Mr Gladstone into the bargain! It's her who should be feeling a twinge of shame, I would say!'

'Hannah, my dear,' Bella protested. Alfie's glance was a grateful one.

'I am only saying what I felt, confused as it might be. Pity is better, perhaps.'

'Was she alone?' Philip continued.

'No, sir. The crowd that were round her had followed her from somewhere else, I would say.'

'These clothes,' the novelist in Bella murmured. 'They sound something of a mare's nest.'

'They were! And I forgot to say, she had bare feet.'

'Did she recognise you?' Philip asked.

'I kept well back,' Alfie promised. 'But if you ask me did I recognise *her*, the answer is yes. Ten times over, yes.'

'Did you follow her?'

'No,' Alfie muttered, blushing.

'You didn't think to follow her?' Bella cried.

'He is not our servant, Bella,' Philip objected, perhaps just a little too sharply. Alfie looked from one to the other in crimson confusion.

'I have a fair idea of where she was headed. And not far at that.'

'St Bart's,' Urmiston guessed at once. 'Isn't the hospital just across the road? Wasn't that where she was going?'

'You're in the right of it, Mr Urmiston. The kitchens end of it anyway. There's as many as fifty

233

wait there all day long for the food bins to be put outside. The scraps, the vegetable peelings and such like. Sometimes scrag ends of meat, even.'

Hannah Bardsoe hauled herself up and fetched the Martinique rum from a side table. It was her indication that the story had taken a sombre turn.

'Then, like you, Alfie dear, I feel pity for the poor soul. It's a pound to a penny she sleeps rough and that will pull a body down faster than a fox in the chicken run. I don't say she should 'scape justice but she's headed for a terrible end nonetheless. I can say this without Billy Murch being present: leave us not forget poor old Molly Clunn and how she finished up.'

'Molly Clunn?' Alfie asked, bewildered. When Bella ruffled his hair, he was amazed to see her eyes filled with tears.

'Someone far more precious to us than the Gollinge woman.'

It was a very awkward moment, for all the way through the table had deferred to Philip Westland as being the arbiter of what should be done in the present instance. The fire crackled and the German case-clock ticked.

'You realise, Alfie,' Philip said in the same gentle voice he had used throughout, 'that the police have been looking for Lady Gollinge with a view to arresting her?'

'Mr Urmiston and me have discussed that from time to time.'

'Did you think to tell a policeman what you had seen in Cock Lane?'

'I wished I need tell no one, sir, and that's no lie. All that whole story has blowed away, to speak frank with you. I was only ever at the edge of it anyroad—and a boy into the bargain. I could see she were a monster all right but hoped never to hear tell of her again. Out of sight, out of mind.'

'But you did tell *me*,' Urmiston observed. 'And I honour you for it. For the rest of us round this table, putting her out of mind is not quite so easy.'

'And I wonder why that is,' Philip Westland said very unexpectedly. His tone was quiet and reflective. 'Do you think she has been punished enough—is that it, Alfie?'

'I think she has come to where she was headed all along, sir. If the police or anyone else wants her, she is not hard to find. Mrs Wallis might like to give her shins a good kicking and if she killed Raybould like they say she did, then I suppose she must pay. But I must tell you plainly, I wish I had not seen her, no, nor never again.'

'You have washed your hands of her,' Bella suggested.

'I have my own life to lead,' Alfie said with great simplicity.

Philip Westland rose from the table and excused himself from the company, saying he would welcome a short turn in the fresh air before it came full dark. To Bella he added that if she could make her way home, he would see her there shortly. Meanwhile, the toasted cheese snack a thing he would like to see introduced as Sunday ritual in Orange Street; hoped, however, they had not inconvenienced Hannah too much on this particular Sabbath. To Urmiston, he expressed the sentiment that they should meet more frequently, perhaps for a chophouse supper. For Alfie Stannard, nothing but a firm, dry and wordless handshake. And then he was gone.

235

'Have I said something wrong?' Alfie asked, bewildered. Bella walked round the table to him and hugged him, before stooping and kissing him on the cheek, dangerously close to his lips.

'You have said something that may turn out to be very important,' she said. And then, as if realising her first kiss might be construed as ambiguous, she kissed him again full on the lips, a thing he would remember for the rest of his life.

* * *

Philip was waiting at the corner of Eagle Street when Alfie walked home. The pair of them were like African explorers meeting in the middle of nowhere, Philip going so far as to shake hands and feeling very fatuous about it, too.

'I could not be sure which way you might come,' he explained. 'But I wanted to talk to you for a few minutes, if you can spare the time.'

'Will you not step up to my room?' the boy asked. 'You can be my first visitor. Until I met Mrs Wallis, I had never tasted coffee and didn't make much of it. But Arthur has shown me how to make it in a jug and Sunday is my day for having some.'

'A cup of coffee would go down very well,' Philip promised.

The stairs to the lodging house were lit as far as the third floor by fluttering gas brackets; but to reach the attics, Philip tramped after his host in single file. He stood patient as a horse in total darkness while Alfie opened up the room and fussed about looking for matches and candles.

'I have a paraffin lamp but it ran dry last night. The smell you have is from something dead under the floorboards.'

'A rat perhaps.'

'I should think so,' Alfie agreed. 'But anyway, welcome to my home.'

'Alfie, I had better say no to coffee,' Philip said after a glance at the tiny grate and its embers, the wall of cardboard boxes and the single rush chair. 'For what I have to ask will take no more than a few minutes of your time and in any case Mrs Wallis will be waiting on me.'

'It is about Lady Gollinge, I suppose?'

'Indirectly.'

He went to the little square window and looked out, his hands blinkering his eyes. Nightfall had jostled the chimney pots into some semblance of a watching crowd, a fancy made all the stronger for the extreme quiet to be had only fifty feet above the pavements. Above the roofline was a clear night sky, with its own attendant watchers. Some of the constellations were vaguely familiar to Philip from the days of his childhood.

'Has Mr Urmiston been to see you here?' he asked.

'Not yet.'

'He would be very sorry to see what he had brought you to, after the open Yorkshire moors.'

'He is not a country man,' Alfie laughed. 'Besides, I like it here well enough for the time being. When I have enough money set by I shall rent a little premises and then you shall see me go.'

'I believe you,' Philip said.

He examined the rush chair as a place to sit and then rejected it in favour of the bed behind the door as a place to watch Alfie rekindle the fire. The fresh coals came from a paper sack and were

237

measured out like sugar lumps.

'Mrs Wallis thinks you are a very gifted young man, Alfie.'

'Meeting her was the best thing that ever happened to me, sir. This is all a bit arse about face—this place, I mean, not London—but I do count myself a lucky lad.'

'You have found yourself,' Philip suggested.

'That is top and bottom of it.'

'I envy you.'

To his amazement, Alfie rounded on him, in so far as it was possible for a boy with a piece of coal in his hand, crouching over an unwilling fire.

'Mr Westland, if there is a luckier man than you from here to China I should like to meet him.'

Which was how it came about that Philip, speaking slowly and addressing the most part of his remarks to his boots, told Alfie the story of Jane Westland and her connections to Ursula Gollinge, the despair he felt at seeing her sink into madness, the guilt that came as a consequence. Alfie heard him out without comment, as though listening to a tragedian's soliloquy, or a prisoner's confession. When Philip faltered to a halt, the silence between them was very long indeed.

'And now,' Alfie suggested, 'you have the lady at your mercy. It would take us no more than an hour to find her, London being what it is, and then you could—well, then you could do whatever you wanted to her.'

'Or I could do what you did, and walk away.'

Philip stood and cracked his knuckles, wandering across to the window again and staring out into the dark. After a moment or two he closed his eyes.

'What did you come up here to ask me, Mr Westland?' Alfie murmured.

'I don't know,' Philip said truthfully enough. 'But it has been worth the journey. More than you realise for the moment, my dear friend. Yes, I will call you that, Alfie. A very dear and unexpected friend.'

*   *   *

Sister Tilde told Mother Superior and she slept on the problem for two nights. Then Tilde was summoned. The two *religieuses* sat in shade, watching the little fountain that burbled not very convincingly in the cloistered part of the asylum. Mother Superior was a tall rangy woman with not too much of the spiritual about her but a great deal of common sense. It was as though the madness of others had licked her into staggering matter-of-factness. It was this that distraught relatives seized upon in gratitude when they had their first interview with her. She had never been seen to smile and that somehow communicated itself to weeping mothers as a further reassurance. Men—fathers, uncles, sons—noticed her huge hands and determined jaw, from which sprang formidable yellowed teeth. Her speech was coarse and direct, unmistakably Parisian in accent. Though it was no part of Tilde's business to hold a personal opinion on her Mother Superior, she admired her enormously.

'Perhaps you will explain what the Englishman hopes to achieve from this particular visit? Has he not tried with his sister before? And were not the consequences—I mean in the short term—

239

disastrous?'

'He believes he has something to say now that Jane has been waiting to hear.'

Mother Superior's glance was slashingly quizzical.

'Tilde, you are not getting sentimental in your old age? The knight in shining armour riding to the rescue at the eleventh hour? I do not think it our business to stage-manage an opera.'

'I have never seen one.'

'This business about a curse is more suited to the stage, nonetheless. You don't believe it, of course?'

'I believe that she believes it.'

A novitiate of the order came out with a glass of lemonade on a wooden tray. Mother Superior took it and drank it off like a workman from Belleville, banging the empty glass back down on the tray.

'Well,' she said. 'Tell him he may come. You may also tell him with suitable asperity that all correspondence is normally addressed to me in the first instance.'

'He is very naive,' Tilde agreed tactfully. 'But his heart is in the right place and he loves his sister as a brother should.'

'Is there money involved? An inheritance, for example?'

But the Mother Superior regretted saying these flinty words as soon as they were spoken. She rose and pulled Tilde up by her wrist.

'You have got me at it now. Tell him to come, with my blessing. If he's as naive as you say he is, he'll turn up on the one day in July likely to cause us the most problems.'

In the men's wing, the twenty or so inmates were

practising the Marseillaise, all of them doleful except for M. Dieumegard, a local man from Rouillac, and a former soldier. His stentorian tenor was champagne to the soul.

* * *

The Quatorze Juillet concert of inmates was held in the little cobbled courtyard that was in front of the main conventual building. A hundred chairs were set out with that French instinct for propriety that is worth more than rubies. They faced a small stage (later to be struck down and returned to the owners of a tivoli who intended it for dancing that night) decorated with chains of flowers. Philip Westland was noticeable in the audience for his great height and the shocking informality of his clothes—a linen suit and soft collar. That year, the average height set for compulsory service in the military was a little over five feet four: the giant Englishman loomed over his neighbours.

The concert was surprisingly good. A man and two women played accordion trios; half a dozen of the women inmates performed country dances in clogs; M. Tixier gave his annual sketch of a farmer trying to teach a dog to jump through hoops, all the patter delivered in a Charentais accent that had the audience in stitches. Mme Paridol sang; M. Lievremont juggled five oranges. The event concluded with the singing of the Marseillaise by all the inmates. Except one. Jane Westland, put in the front row for her pale beauty, did not open her mouth. Her head was cocked as if listening to another music altogether, as if carried on the air from another country.

241

At the end of the concert, the inmates filed away to their lunch and once they were safely locked inside, the courtyard gates were opened. Philip walked to the park bench Tilde the Belgian had picked out for him and waited patiently for two hours. Then and only then he came face to face with Jane. Tilde watched as without a word he passed his sister cuttings from three London newspapers.

'Is it true?' she asked.

'She was buried eight days ago. Yes, it is true. I went to the service. At Brookwood.'

'Where is that?'

'Near Woking. It is the largest cemetery in the world.'

Jane Westland crumpled the cuttings in her fist and let them fall to the ground.

'Who paid?'

'We do not know. It doesn't matter.'

'Did she suffer?'

'I think she did.'

'But we ought not to talk like that,' Tilde chided gently, taking Jane's hand.

'She did not suffer the way you have been made to suffer,' Philip persisted. 'But she lost everything. I believe that, Jane. All her powers.'

'Can't she speak from the grave?'

'In Woking?' Philip asked and was rewarded with a short smile that skipped the years of madness and went all the way back to their shared childhood.

'This is my brother,' she told Tilde.

Philip took both Jane's hands and brought them to his lips.

'And this is my beloved sister.'

In 1933, Alfred Stannard died at his home in Thames Ditton, a sprawling mock-Tudor house with long lawns leading to the river. He left behind a philately business worth several hundred thousand pounds, and a personal stamp collection that took two days to dispose of at auction. Stannard was seventy-one when he died. He never married. Three of the many obituaries garnered at his death mentioned that he was among the last of the Victorians, occasioning a characteristically bombastic rejoinder from George Bernard Shaw, who was four years older and perhaps a hundred times more arrogant.

Among his papers was the original of a much reprinted photograph of the original Stannard shop, a tiny property in Fleur de Lys Court. The proprietor is seen as a very young man, standing with a woman far too carelessly described as his mother. The lady in question is Hannah Bardsoe, the only likeness that ever existed of her. Some historians believe this second figure to be his first customer; or more fancifully still, his financial backer. The truth is simpler. Urmiston, who took the photograph, had Hannah's black canvas shopping bag at his feet. Inside, was a celebratory veal-and-ham pie and—for luck—a sprig of Yorkshire heather.

In his lifetime, Stannard published three books, all of them to do with philately. In between the pages of what is still a standard text on the plating of the Queen Victoria Penny Red, the auctioneers found the order of service of Mrs Arabella Wallis's wedding to Mr Philip Westland, which took place at St George's Hanover Square in 1878. Across the top of the folded sheet, in a woman's hand, were written the words '*To my dearest darling Alfie, with love from us both.*' As happens with ink, the superscription had grown faint and ghostly. But then ink is never the whole story. The whole story, like the whole world, is unknowable.